the REPRISE

CONNOR BRYAN

Sun Cat
Publishing

This is a work of fiction. All characters, organizations, and events portrayed in this novel are either products of the author's imagination or are used fictitiously.

First paperback edition February 2023

Book design by Connor Bryan

ISBN 979-8-9864849-1-4 (trade paperback)

Published by Sun Cat Publishing

To all the a cappella geeks out there who loved *Pitch Perfect* just a little too much.

CHAPTER 1
PRESENT

Knock, knock.

Who's there?

An idiot in a sunhat.

There he stands: Wesley, looking like a Greek god in swim trunks, dark skin glistening under his liberal application of sunscreen, with a floppy, wide-brimmed hat, a big beach bag over one shoulder, and a suitcase handle clutched in one hand.

Quinn doesn't miss the way he grips it tighter as soon as Wesley sees them.

"Um... hey," Wesley says, awkward and awful.

Quinn doesn't even answer. They just turn away and head back to the small sofa, a fort protecting them from the man in the doorway.

Why did Dove have to invite him?

"Wesley!" Dove says in her patented sing-song voice.

"Hey!" Wesley greets her, much more upbeat and amicable now.

The others wander over as Wesley steps inside and closes the door behind him. Carina, a tall, olive-skinned woman wearing red-tinted sunglasses, glances at Quinn from where she stands in the small kitchen. Her gaze clearly says both, 'You okay?' and 'Play nice.'

Wesley continues greeting the rest of their friends. It figures he'd be happier to see everyone else than he is to see Quinn.

Quinn can't really blame him though.

"So this place… is nice," Wesley lies.

"Oh em gee, Wes, no," Dove says. "I swear it doesn't look like its Airbnb pictures. I didn't choose this place on purpose."

Something skitters through the attic and everyone glances up.

"Well, I think it's great," Basil says. She was their alto when they sung together, and it shows in her voice. Soft, low, and rich. And shy. Altos are shy.

It's Basil's birthday in just a couple days. That's why they're all here. Dove orchestrated this grand reunion of their a cappella club to celebrate. Their group, A Cademia—like 'a cappella' and 'academia'—broke up four months ago, but apparently, Dove doesn't care about that. She apparently also doesn't care about the lasting tension between Quinn and Wesley.

Dove didn't care to inform Quinn of everyone that was going to be attending. Quinn only had about a ten-minute warning before Wesley arrive, and from the shocked look on Wesley's face, Quinn would guess he found out exactly when Quinn answered the door.

Quinn peers over the back of the couch as Dove shows Wesley to his room.

Carina leans over the sofa and says, "Boo."

Quinn glares at her and lets their head fall back against the arm of the couch, which they thought would be much softer.

"You okay?" Carina asks.

"Yeah. I'm not mad anymore or anything."

"You sure?" she asks pointedly.

"Uh, yeah? Why?"

"You're scowling like someone just told you that digital's better than film."

"No, I'm not," Quinn insists. Then consciously unclenches their fists. Maybe they are a little mad.

It's not their fault. Anyone would be mad, both at what Wesley did and at the situation at hand. Being stuck with your ex isn't fun and being stuck with them in a tiny beach cottage starting on the stormiest day the Keys have seen in a while isn't fun either.

Quinn groans. "Tell me it's gonna be fine."

Carina doesn't. Instead, she says, "Have you counted the rooms?"

Quinn sits up and looks at her like she just asked them to solve her riddles three. What is this, a brain teaser? "No, I haven't counted the rooms."

"Do that." She drums on the couch and walks back into the kitchen to continue nursing her margarita.

Quinn tilts their head to squint down the short hallway. One, two... and that door leads to a bathroom. Their face goes slack with realization. There are six of them on this trip.

There are two rooms. There's a good chance they and Wesley might room together.

Speak of the devil. He and Dove emerge from the leftmost room.

When Quinn arrived an hour ago, Dove took their backpack and suitcase for them while Quinn greeted the rest of the group.

Quinn better not be rooming with Wesley.

"Dove," Quinn whispers, "Dove!"

She looks up, then spots the source of the whispering. "Hey, what's up?" she whispers back.

"Which room am I in?"

Dove raises her eyebrows and tightens her lips into a playful face, feigning innocence. "I dunno."

"Dove, come on."

"Here's a tip, Canon," she says, pulling out an old nickname, "RSVP next time. That way, the host might consider your lodging requests. Have fun."

"I texted you!" Quinn insists.

"Mm-hm. Yesterday."

"Yeah!" They don't see anything wrong with that.

"Bye, Quinn," Dove says as she walks around the couch, through the small living area, and to the sliding glass door.

She slides it open and steps outside. Her clothes and hair start whipping around in the wind, and Quinn notices how dark it is outside for 3 PM. Dove immediately comes back inside. "Yeah, no." She slides her hands through her curly, natural hair and smooths it back down. Somehow, she still looks angelic. That's sopranos for you.

"Now that we're all here… is it about time to do some shots?" Quinn looks over and sees Eddie standing in the kitchen. He has a necktie tied around his forehead as if he's been at a rager, not an a cappella club reunion.

The rest of their friends cheer and rush to the counter, banging on it and chanting, "Shots! Shots! Shots!" Even sweet little Basil joins in even though she can't and won't drink yet.

Eddie pours everyone a shot in adorable mini red Solo cups that Quinn has the intense urge to make into earrings.

"Quinn, come on!" Dove says, gesturing for Quinn to join them.

Grudgingly, they stand and walk over, ending up between Basil and Carina.

Eddie passes out shots and hands Basil a shot of Capri Sun. "Happy birthday to you," Eddie starts singing as if Basil's Capri Sun shot is a cake.

Eddie's needlessly dramatic rendition ends, and everyone takes their shots and slams their cups down on the counter. Dove and Basil cheer and dance around, and Quinn can't help but smile at their ridiculous friends.

Quinn's lucky to have them, and to still have them. They've heard lots of stories about people losing their friend groups after breakups. These were all Wesley's friends first. Quinn admittedly doesn't have the easiest time making new friends, probably due to their perpetual scowl and sardonic sense of humor—if it can be called humor—it's mostly morbid jokes and cynicism. If they lost these people, they wouldn't have anyone else.

Quinn thinks back to their semesters before joining the a cappella group. They remember how lonely they were, sitting off to one side in every class, walking out of the classroom silently at the end. Even if people showed mild interest in being their friend, they'd act cold and weird and shut them out. No one usually stuck around after that.

Quinn was so resentful of Wesley at first, for making them join his stupid club. But now, looking around at these people taking more shots (and Basil drinking more Capri Sun), they actually feel a pang of guilt for being so cold to him. He may have destroyed Quinn's heart a few months ago, but he still gave them these wonderful people. Their gaze shifts to Wesley, still shirtless in his swim trunks as he laughs with the others, but Quinn looks away before they accidentally make eye contact.

Then their gaze hardens again, and they shoot lasers into the countertop. No. Quinn hasn't forgotten what Wesley did, what he said. No way on Earth is Quinn ever going to be grateful to him.

CHAPTER 2
PAST

Why are words so difficult? Quinn sits staring at their blinking cursor, as they try to come up with something called a 'thesis statement'. They don't know which demon of hell created such a thing, but it must have been one of the worst, because who else could come up with torture so sinister?

Quinn writes: *Public transportation is good because it is good for the earth and for the people on public transportation because they don't have to drive.*

They lean their chair back on two legs and let out a loud groan.

This is impossible. Quinn's glad they don't have to turn in the whole research paper at once, but if just the thesis statement is this hard, Quinn shudders to think how difficult the next stage is going to be—the annotated bibliography. Quinn only knows one of those words, and just barely.

They delete the sentence they wrote and stare at the empty page again. Without thinking, they let out another groan.

"Hey," a voice says from behind them a few moments later. They look up and see a guy around Quinn's age. He has closely cropped hair and a wide smile displaying a row of perfect teeth. "Hi. Yeah. I just wanted to remind you that this is a library, and people are studying, so if you could keep it down, that'd be wonderful."

Oh, he's an asshole.

Quinn makes a sarcastic face. "Uh-huh. Thanks so much for letting me know."

The man's eyebrows shoot up. "No need for the attitude."

"I could say the same." Quinn now sees the guy is wearing his student ID on his lanyard. Nerd. His name is Wesley, apparently.

Wesley glances at Quinn's empty document on the screen. "I see you're making a lot of progress over here."

"Okay, asshole. You try writing a thesis statement about your stance on public transportation if it's so easy."

"A wave of the future, public transportation can provide many benefits, including increased safety due to fewer vehicles on the road, lower carbon emissions, and cheaper transportation costs for individuals."

Okay, damn. That's pretty good for an asshole. "What are you, a tutor?"

Wesley rolls his eyes. "Just keep it down, okay?" He turns and walks back to his study carrel by the window.

Oh shit. Bubble butt.

Quinn pretends they didn't notice that. That's embarrassing.

They try to remember what Wesley had said and jot it down, but they can't quite remember everything. They come up with: *Public transportation is good because it is a wave of the future, it is safer because there are no cars, and*

They can't think of the rest. Quinn eyes his study carrel. They could walk over there and ask him to repeat himself. It'd be so easy. Then they'd have this assignment done.

No. Wesley was rude from the start. Quinn's not gonna go over there and inflate his ego even further.

Quinn can do it themself.

♪♪♪

They do not end up doing it themself.

Quinn gets yet another zero for a missing assignment, because 'couldn't do it' didn't turn out to be a valid excuse.

They now have nearly a failing grade in English. You know, the language they speak.

To shake off the awful feeling of failing yet another assignment, Quinn puts on their headphones and starts on a long walk around the campus.

Their playlist is a chaotic mix of 2014 emo boy bands, Paramore, and old Avril Lavigne. As Quinn walks with their hands plunged in the pockets of their denim jacket they thrifted in ninth grade, they hum an emo deepcut.

The thrumming baseline and impossibly quick percussion brings feeling back to their fingertips as if Quinn is the one giving the drums all they've got.

These songs got them through high school, and apparently, Quinn hasn't changed as much as they'd like to think, because the same songs are carrying them through college, too.

The Copper Cove University campus is pretty beautiful. Amidst the historic stone buildings, there are lots of green areas, from small patches of landscaping beside entrances, to full parks where students sit on blankets eating lunch or studying beneath the trees. A pathway snakes through the middle of one such park and Quinn takes it, singing what they think could possibly be the correct lyrics to the Fall Out Boy song. They can't ever quite tell what the singer is saying.

The bridge of the song transitions into an intense hook which leads into a powerful chorus and Quinn can't help but sing along quietly. At least, they hope it's quiet. They can't always tell with their headphones on.

Quinn's walk is going well, with a slight breeze in the air and the sun hiding behind the clouds, but it doesn't go well for long. Suddenly, someone grabs their arm and Quinn knocks their headphones down around their neck. It's Wesley, and he's saying something. "—voice."

Quinn assumes he's reprimanding them for their volume again. "Are you kidding me?" they say. "You're telling me to keep it down *outside?*"

"What? No. I said you have a beautiful voice."

"I—oh, okay. Thanks?" *Bubble butt likes my voice… Nice.*

Wesley squints, an idea obviously forming in his head. "Hey…"

Quinn doesn't want to hear another word that comes out of his mouth, so they move to put their headphones back on, but Wesley stops them.

"What if I tutor you in English? I know you need the help."

"I do not."

"What'd you get on your thesis statement?"

"I... didn't do it."

Wesley raises his eyebrows as if to say, 'Exactly.' He continues, "I'll tutor you in English if you join the CCU a cappella club."

"A cappella?" Quinn stares at him blankly. "You mean, like 'Pitch Perfect'?"

Wesley grapples with that statement for a moment, then comes up with, "I don't know what that is."

Okay, so Quinn is *definitely* not joining that club. "Thanks, but no thanks." They start to put their headphones on and once again Wesley stops them.

"You're in Comp 2, right? Who do you have?"

"Duke."

"I had her too. You're about to have a test on the three novels you guys read, right?"

"Right. Books that we read..."

"You didn't even read them?" Wesley asks, as if any college student reads the assigned novels. Quinn stares at him blankly. Wesley shakes his head and refocuses. "Okay, anyway—you need my help, and we need a tenor."

"Tenor?"

"Yeah. That's the vocal part your voice is."

"Why can't you just find someone else?"

"No one else will join." Wesley doesn't give Quinn time to unpack that, continuing, "Come on. Just think about it, okay?"

He looks awfully earnest, eyes wide and almost desperate. Quinn raises their eyebrows and puts their headphones back on. "Don't count on it."

How dare Wesley imply that Quinn will fail their test without him? Sure, they didn't read *Lord of the Flies* or that weird Shakespeare play about fairies, but they can get through this just fine. How hard can it be?

Hard. Extremely.

This test becomes yet another failure. They earned a 64% which actually does bring their grade up by a couple hundredths of a point, but that's depressing all on its own.

Quinn is in the library working on their bibliography. They now understand what it is, but they still have no clue where to start. Despite themself, they glance up at the study carrel by the big window.

No. They can't give in like that. They can't let Wesley win.

But it's either that or fail another class.

Ugh.

Quinn stuffs their notebook back into their backpack and trudges over. "Fine," Quinn mutters.

Wesley spins in his chair—hey, where'd he get a spinny chair?—and looks at Quinn smugly. "You'll join the group?"

Quinn tugs on their backpack strap. "Yep."

"And you'll take it seriously? No lip-syncing, no skipping practices?"

"Bye." Quinn turns around but Wesley shoots out a hand to grab their arm.

"Hang on. Do you want help or not?"

Quinn glares at him, but Wesley takes it as a yes.

"So do we have a deal?" Wesley holds out his hand.

Quinn rolls their eyes and shakes it. "Whatever."

"Great!" Wesley says, chipper. "First practice is tomorrow morning at 8. See you then."

Quinn's jaw drops. "8 in the morning? My first class is at 12. What am I supposed to do for, like, three hours?"

"Practices are two hours long, first of all. And second, we can study." Wesley smiles like he means it, but Quinn doesn't know how he could. He must be an academic sadist.

Quinn makes a mental note to set their alarm four hours earlier than normal. This is gonna suck.

CHAPTER 3
PRESENT

Quinn loves their friends but hates them drunk. Dove sings pop songs too high-pitched, then gets sad and sobs into Carina's shoulder. Eddie loses all impulse control, of which he has very little under normal circumstances, let alone drunk. Wesley dances annoyingly well to anything that's playing. Once, at Dove's own birthday party back in March, the playlist got mixed up and Dove's opera started playing. Quinn had no idea you could twerk to an aria about despair.

Lucky for Quinn, Carina stays the exact same when drunk—which does make them wonder if she is always drunk—and Basil can't drink yet, so the three of them sit on the couch while the others make fools of themselves.

Carina sips on her Old Fashioned, which—gross. "Watch this," she says, then she stands and walks over to Eddie in the kitchen. "I dare you to eat whatever's in the freezer."

Eddie smiles, perplexed. "Um, 'kay, but *we* stocked the fridge so it's, like, pizzas and french fries and stuff."

"No," Carina says. "What was *left* in the freezer."

"What? Like... like what the last people left behind?"

Carina nods, her eyes glinting and her smile sharp at the edges.

Quinn knows Eddie won't turn down a dare, especially after four Whiteclaws.

Eddie nods and shakes out his arms. "What do I get if I win?"

"Nothing."

Eddie tilts his head to one side and thinks before saying, "Eh, alright." He opens the fridge and roots around until he exclaims, "Ew! No way."

Something even Eddie thinks is gross? It must be something truly awful. Quinn's gotta see this. They and Basil walk over as everyone crowds around. Even Wesley has stopped dancing.

Eddie pulls out a vacuum-sealed pouch. Its contents are mostly obscured by the dense, foggy frost that has spread across the bag. Eddie scrapes some ice off with his thumb and it reveals the label: Sailor Jim's Bait.

"No way," Quinn says, laughing. "How did you know that was in there?" they ask Carina.

"Lucky guess," she replies.

"Guys," Eddie says, looking to his friends for sympathy. "We don't have to—You guys don't wanna see me eat this. Let's just call this off, huh?"

"You agreed to the dare," Carina says.

"I know, but—"

"A Cademia bylaws state that if a dare is accepted but not accomplished, the daree must do the bidding of the darer until the terms of the dare are fulfilled."

"You don't mean—"

"Eat the fish, Edward." As soon as Eddie looks away, she smirks sinisterly.

Eddie opens the pouch and braces himself for the smell, but because it's frozen, it doesn't have a scent. That's one tiny win for Eddie, at least. The group watches as he fishes out a fish and inspects it. "It's got eyes, guys. *Eyes.*"

"Eat the fish," Carina chants. "Eat the fish." Everyone joins in and Quinn is glad this Airbnb is a shack without nearby neighbors because oh boy, do a cappella singers know how to project their voices.

Eddie leans his head back and holds the fish over his mouth, lowers it in headfirst, and bites it with a sickening *crunch*.

He chews it and it keeps crunching and cracking. Quinn tells themself it's just because it's frozen... not because of the head.

Eddie forces himself to swallow, then sticks out his tongue, still littered with fish bits, but it's unmistakable; he ate the head.

The group cheers and Eddie dances around calling himself the Bait King. What a sad kingdom he rules.

Quinn smirks, then sees Carina wink at them. Did she do this just to cheer them up? Either way, it worked.

"Who's up for some night swimming?" Dove shouts.

"Uh... Isn't that kind of dangerous? You guys are really drunk," Quinn points out.

"We're not *that* drunk," Dove says.

"Eddie's drunk enough that he just bit the head off a fish," Quinn says, gesturing to the Bait King.

Dove waves the idea away. "No, we're fine. Everyone, don thine suits of swimming!"

Everyone heads toward the rooms and Quinn fixes Dove with a calculating look. She wouldn't put them and Wesley in the same room. She knows better than to stoke that fire. But the way she acted earlier makes them think maybe she did put them together, just to be difficult.

Quinn walks into the room on the right, hopeful.

"Hey, bud," Carina says, already in a rash guard and swim shorts.

"Is my stuff in here?"

"No, sorry." Basil turns around from facing the back corner, her swimsuit now safely on, and smiles at Quinn, who smiles back.

Ugh. Why, Dove?

Quinn walks to the next room where Eddie stands completely naked asking Wesley which pair of trunks suits him better. Wesley, who came dressed in his own already, is sitting on the edge of his bed, utterly mortified. He almost looks grateful when Quinn walks in, but Quinn knows better than that.

"Hey, what do you think?" Eddie asks them. Quinn looks at the two swim trunks, one blue with pink flamingos, and the other green with tropical parrots all over it.

"Birds."

Eddie's smile disappears, replaced by tense brows and a deep frown. He mutters to himself, "But they're both birds..."

There are three twin beds, and unfortunately for Quinn, their backpack and suitcase are on the middle one. Dove couldn't even put them on opposite sides of the room?

Quinn grabs their swimsuit out of their suitcase and walks into the bathroom to change. When they emerge, everyone is in the kitchen taking one more round of shots. That's a good plan. Get drunker before going out into the darkness to splash around in volatile water where a riptide could very well be hiding. Smart.

Dove opens the sliding glass door and runs down to the beach, the others running after her.

"Just leaving the door open, huh? Not like mosquitoes carry malaria or anything." Quinn slides the door shut. At least it's stopped raining.

Carina shoots them a look that says, 'Lighten up,' and Quinn scowls at her.

Quinn meets the rest of them at the water's edge. They watch Dove splash around and stop themself from telling her to be careful. Sometimes they feel like they're the only voice of reason in this group. They shouldn't have to feel that way.

If the others get to be carefree on their vacation, Quinn's gonna feel that way too.

They realize they're standing next to Wesley, who makes a face that says he agrees the others are crazy. Quinn shrugs and runs into the water, splashing Dove, who yelps and sends a splash right back.

It's kind of fun being ridiculous. Quinn spares a glance at Wesley, still standing with his feet barely in the water, and feels another unwanted pang of guilt. He looks like he feels left out.

Uh, no. Wesley is the last person Quinn is going to feel guilty for abandoning. Wesley is the one who should feel bad.

No, Quinn, stop. You're not going to think about your breakup on your vacation. It's bad enough that Wesley's even here. You don't have to make it worse by dwelling on the past.

Quinn shakes it off and returns to frolicking in the ocean with their friends. The very dark, very deep, very dangerous ocean.

Okay, maybe Quinn isn't exactly as carefree as their friends are.

CHAPTER 4
PAST

Yeah. A cappella club isn't for them.

Quinn shows up only a few minutes late which is pretty good for them. They walk into a small black box theater with acoustic foam pads on the walls. The sign by the door says Theater B.

"Great, you made it." Wesley jogs over and walks them in. "Everyone, this is Quinn. They're gonna be our tenor." Wesley tells Quinn everyone's names, then walks to the front of the room and practice begins.

"Hi," a girl named Basil whispers. "I'm glad you joined us! You're gonna have a lot of fun."

Quinn gives her a fake smile. Yeah, right.

Wesley leads them in a warm-up, then he passes out a folded booklet of sheet music. It looks really complicated. Quinn used to play piano in middle school so they're familiar with the sheet music itself, but there are five separate melody lines, all with the same words but different notes. Each staff is labeled: soprano, alto, tenor, bass, percussion. How do they find their notes if everyone's singing something different?

Easily, Quinn supposes, because Wesley plays a few notes on the piano, counts them in, and the group starts singing. Quinn looks around like an idiot, not even pretending to know what they're doing.

It sounds nice. Dove's honey-smooth soprano voice complements the others. Eddie is singing the higher harmonies with her but branches out into his own notes every once in a while. Quinn didn't see a staff that matches what Eddie's singing, so either he has a different version of the sheet music, or he's just doing his own thing.

Basil's sweet alto voice is quiet but powerful, and her notes play with Dove's, adding texture and warmth. Wesley's bass voice is rich and clear, and it adds depth to their sound. Carina's got the mouth percussion down, and she can mimic a snare drum exactly.

Where does Quinn fit in here? It seems like they've got all the bases covered. They don't need them.

The song ends, and Wesley says, "So what did you think?"

Dove is the first to answer. "Eh... I think it's okay, but it wouldn't be my first choice for sectionals."

"I haven't heard that song before now," Basil says. "I thought it was pretty good, but yeah, I agree with Dove."

She hadn't heard the song before? Wait... This was a sight read? They hadn't encountered this sheet music until they sang it just now? Yeah, they definitely don't need Quinn. They'll just slow the group down.

Wesley pulls out another stack of sheet music, this time low-quality scans that distorted all the text. Luckily, Quinn actually knows this song. It's 'Fly Me to the Moon' by Frank Sinatra. They played it at their first and only piano recital where they messed up in the middle and just stopped. After that, Quinn's family's piano sat untouched for years until they finally sold it to a kid up the street.

"Tenor has the melody, okay?" Wesley says to Quinn. He plays their notes again, and the song begins. Quinn follows along okay, singing quietly but loud enough for their voice to mix in nicely with the others. They stumble a couple times but manage to find their note and keep going.

Practice ends, and it was surprisingly okay. Quinn quickly discovers they actually don't mind singing. It can be pretty fun, creating a complete sound from silence. They're even thinking they might be able to put up with this, that is, until the next practice when Wesley introduces... *team-building games*.

The next week, Quinn is tasked with catching Dove as she falls backwards into them, and on the sixth trust fall, Quinn decides they're not coming back. They'd actually prefer to fail English at this point.

Practice ends at 10 and Quinn heads to tutoring with Wesley until their next class at 12. They're working on Quinn's annotated bibliography. As they walk to the library, Wesley lists what's left to be done. "And when is it due?" he asks.

"Uh... today?"

"Today?" Wesley exclaims. "You never told me it was due today."

"What the hell? Yes I did."

"No, I think I'd remember if you said—"

"That it's due on Tuesday. I said that last week."

"Huh. Maybe you did," Wesley concedes. "Sorry."

"It's fine." Quinn can tell Wesley is waiting for them to ask him what's wrong. They don't.

That doesn't stop Wesley from sharing, however. "I'm just feeling distracted. You know, sectionals are coming up—"

"What?"

"Sectionals."

"What's that?" Quinn asks.

Wesley stops walking. "Sectionals? The competition that we're going to in three months? The thing we've been working towards? I told you about this."

There's a competition? Quinn is *definitely* not going back. "Okay, you forgot my thing, I forgot yours. I guess we're even."

"Anyway, point is, I'm sorry." They reach the doors to the library and Wesley pulls one open. "I think we should be good to go for your class today. We just need to find one more source and annotate the last three."

Quinn doesn't hate their tutoring sessions with Wesley.

They know that they should, but something about him is just genuinely nice to be around. He cares so much about the

English department that Quinn could almost swear that he cares about Quinn's grade specifically. But Quinn knows he probably has a lot more tutoring students, and they probably all feel that way too. That's just Wesley, Quinn supposes. Caring and genuine.

...seeming. Caring- and genuine-*seeming*. That wasn't a compliment. That was an accusation. Duh.

They finish Quinn's bibliography, and it actually turns out pretty good. Professor Duke seems impressed, but Quinn's not sure if it's the quality of the work or the fact that they turned something in at all.

"Nicely done. Did you have help?" she asks. For once, a teacher asked if they had help and it doesn't sound like an accusation of cheating.

"Yeah, actually. Wesley, a tutor at the student center."

"Wesley," she says fondly and takes off her glasses. "Good student. You said he's a tutor?"

Quinn nods.

"Strange. He used to tutor. It seemed like he enjoyed it. But he decided one day to quit. Never gave a reason. Nice to know he's back at it." Professor Duke goes back to grading papers, so Quinn sits down in their chair at the table in the back.

Hey... Could Quinn be the only person Wesley's tutoring? Could Quinn be an exception? No, that'd be crazy.

Quinn sleeps through the next A Cademia practice and has no regrets. Have fun doing lip trills and singing weird arrangements of Journey songs, losers!

They wake up with their alarm at 10 AM and head to the library, where they sit and wait for fifteen minutes at Wesley's study carrel. He's never been late before. Practice must have run long. Quinn's glad this is the one they decided to skip.

Five minutes later, a student librarian walks over with a sticky note. "Wesley told me to give you this."

"He was here?" Quinn asks, taking the note.

"Yeah, just a minute ago." She walks away and Quinn frowns.

The note says, *No practice, no tutoring.*

Oh, come on. It was one practice.

Quinn can admit the tutoring really has been helping. They're firmly at a passing grade now in English, and that annotated bibliography should help too. But who says they need to be tutored by Wesley? There are plenty of English tutors at this school, hell, in this *room*. They can have their pick of the litter. Who needs that guy?

♩♪♪

That doesn't go so well. The first tutor Quinn tries is a stern, blonde girl with a permanent line etched between her eyebrows. Whenever Quinn makes a typo, she jabs at the computer screen until they fix it.

The next tutor is even worse. Quinn thought he was great at first, but they soon realize every compliment is backhanded and every correction is an insult. "Wow, nice. That's such a long word," he'd say, or, "Nope, no comma there. My bad, I thought we were in college."

That doesn't last long, but they were the only student-center-endorsed tutors available. After struggling with the rough draft of their research paper the night before, Quinn decides to make use of the college's bulletin board.

> *need tutor for english pls*
>
> *text me*

Hopefully that will get some bites. Quinn thinks the abbreviation of 'please' might be enough to snare a grammar freak.

They'll just have to wait and see.

CHAPTER 5
PRESENT

The group comes in from the beach and simultaneously has the realization there's only one bathroom and six sandy people.

Quinn books it for the shower and ends up second in line after Basil, who closes the door just in time. Quinn grabs a change of clothes and Basil doesn't take too long, so soon enough Quinn is able to rinse off their sandy legs.

Quinn walks back into their room, pajamas on and looking forward to a restful night. They ignore Wesley who is sitting on the edge of his own bed waiting for his turn in the shower. Quinn sits down and pulls the covers up.

"Wes, your turn," Dove calls.

Wesley leaves the room and as soon as he's out of earshot, Eddie turns toward Quinn and says, "Dish."

"Dish? Ed, you were around when it all went down."

"I know, but there has to be more to the story. The lingering looks, the tension. Are you feeling that spark again?"

"There is no spark. Never was," Quinn says, a little sadder than they meant to sound.

"Aw, well maybe it'll come back."

"No," Quinn says forcefully. "I don't want it back. I don't want him back."

Eddie raises his hands to say he's innocent. "Okay, okay. But if you need to talk about it, I'm here."

"You mean if I need to dish."

"Exactly. What'd I say?"

Quinn rolls their eyes and grins. Eddie's ridiculous, but he always makes Quinn smile.

After a few minutes, Wesley returns in just a towel and Eddie wolf whistles while Quinn averts their eyes. After putting on shorts, Wesley tosses his towel at Eddie and it lands on his head.

Eddie pulls it off and hugs it to his chest. "Thank you, Wesley. I'll treasure it always."

Wesley laughs and rolls his eyes like Quinn had.

Eddie strikes up a conversation with Wesley about their favorite movies. Eddie says anything Marvel, and Wesley says anything Wes Andersen. Eddie says it's just because they're both named Wes.

Quinn gets up so quickly they bump the table and the lamp teeters. They steady it before walking out of the room. An echo from four months ago ricochets around their head.

'Wes—'

'Don't call me that.'

The couch is looking pretty good right about now but they stop short when they see it's already taken by Carina.

"Hey, kiddo." She pats the cushion next to her and Quinn sits.

They're silent for a few moments before Quinn blurts, "I don't wanna talk about it."

Carina lets that hang for a beat, then says, "Okay."

Only, Quinn does wanna talk about it. They want to get all this off their chest, they want to talk about the competition and the camera and everything Wesley said and everything Quinn said and how Quinn would have preferred that it had happened over text so they could carefully write down what they felt instead of everything just exploding out, their mouth an exit wound.

But they don't.

Because they can't. It's Basil's birthday tomorrow and this trip is about her. It would be inconsiderate to air out their own issues in the middle of her celebration. That's why they're going to remain cordial with Wesley, if a bit cold.

♪♪♪

Quinn ends up sleeping on the couch that night after Carina goes to bed, and their neck is not thanking them for the experience. They sit up when the sun streams in through the sliding glass door, a sunbeam settling right over their face. Quinn rolls their head both ways and tries to rub the muscle, but it's no use. They can't get the right angle.

Everyone else gets up not too long after, and Basil notices Quinn's discomfort while they're sitting on the barstools drinking pulpy orange juice together. Quinn doesn't care for pulp, but it's Basil's favorite, so that's what they bought.

"You know," Basil starts, "sometimes for a crick in my neck, if I can get it to crack it goes away."

"I tried that, but it won't crack," Quinn says, their hand still trying and failing to rub out the knot.

"Oh, you know who's great at that is—" Basil cuts herself off and takes a sip of her O.J.

"What?"

"Hm? Oh, um…" Basil leans in. "Well, I was going to say Wesley, but…"

Quinn nods and clutches their glass like it's a beer on a hard day.

Looks like their neck is just going to hurt today.

The group heads out into the town. Their Airbnb is in a small community in the Florida Keys. It has shops and restaurants in a plaza in the center. Basil spots an ice cream shop and drags Quinn by the hand. Quinn gets pistachio of course.

They walk around a few more of the shops, mostly touristy with oyster shells dyed bright pink, starfish with googly eyes, and cheesy wooden signs that say things like *'this way to the beach'* and *'gone fishing'*. One shop claimed to be antiques but is little more than a Florida Keys t-shirt store. They do have a display case of antique film cameras, though. They even have a Canon AE-1 like Quinn used to have. Their stomach ties itself in a knot and they move on, but not before Dove sees them looking at it.

"Aw, remember your camera?" she says.

Of course Quinn does. They nod.

"And we used to call you Canon, aw. Do you still have it?"

"Nope."

They walk out of the store and back into the bright Florida sun. The group heads toward the shade of the gazebo in the center of the plaza.

Quinn stops as soon as they're in the shade and brings their hand to the side of their neck. They try to press down on the knot, but they still can't get the right angle.

"You okay?"

Quinn glances at Wesley. "Fine."

"Neck?"

"Yes," Quinn grits.

"Need help—"

"No." Though, the memory of Wesley's strong hands gently massaging the pain from Quinn's shoulders is— entirely unwelcome. That's what it is.

Always the master of perfect timing, Dove exclaims, "Look at this!" from where she stands in front of a town bulletin board. "A couple days from now is the 6th Annual Conch Republic Music Jamboree."

"Cool," Wesley says, walking closer.

"And"—Dove gasps—"singing competition!" She whips around to face the rest of the group. "Guys…"

"No way," Quinn says.

"Why not?" Dove asks.

"We don't even live here. Why would we perform in their competition?" Quinn points out.

"Well… because we're really good," Basil chimes in.

"I say we do it," Eddie says.

Wesley nods, and Quinn looks at Carina who nods too.

"Birthday girl has spoken, I guess," Quinn says.

Dove and Basil cheer, and Carina takes a picture of the flier.

"Oh shit," Carina says, pointing at the poster. "Did you even notice the prize?"

The five of them crowd around and look over her shoulder. The grand prize is a three-night stay at a condo on the beach. There are two small photos and from what Quinn can see, it looks really nice. But after arriving at the tiny, broken-down shack, they've learned not to trust pictures of beach houses.

"Guys, this is perfect!" Dove says. "The prize is three days, right? We have five days left of our trip. If we win this condo stay at the Jamboree two days from now, we can spend the rest of the time at the condo instead of that dinky Airbnb."

"That's a great idea!" Basil says. "But honestly, I really don't mind the shack. I think it's nice you guys came to celebrate at all. I don't care where we stay!"

Eddie ruffles Basil's short brown hair and it falls into her eyes.

"So it's settled," Wesley says. "We'll spend the next couple days practicing, and then we'll try to win the prize."

"No, we won't try to win," Carina says. "We *will* win."

Quinn likes her confidence, but their group hasn't performed together in half a year. Quinn hasn't even sung at all in that time.

"A Cademia on three," Wesley says, thrusting his hand out. They all add their hands to the center, and he counts, "One... two... three!"

They each hit their note. Well, no, they each hit *a* note. This used to be their club cheer—sing their club's name in harmony. This time, it's less harmonious and more dissonant, but after a moment they fall into their proper pitches, and it actually sounds nice. It reminds Quinn of old times.

Too bad those old times suck.

CHAPTER 6
PAST

So, the note pinned to the bulletin board did not work out. No one called Quinn, and then it got ripped down. Quinn has no idea who would do such a thing until they spot the piece of paper at Wesley's study carrel.

Quinn marches over. "Hey, asshole."

Wesley turns. "That's a little aggressive, don't you think?"

Quinn ignores him and snatches the piece of paper off his desk and waves it around. "What the hell is this, huh? Why do you have this?"

Wesley spins his chair to face Quinn fully and says, "Yeah, I was meaning to talk to you about that."

"About what? About you abandoning me?"

Wesley gets a line across his forehead. "I didn't abandon you, Quinn. We had a deal, and I was reminding you that it's a two-way street." Wesley reaches out and takes the paper from Quinn. "You'd really rather resort to this than sing with us?"

Quinn stays quiet, a deep scowl heavy on their face.

"Really?" Wesley nudges.

"It's just not for me. The singing and stuff. You guys are really good at it and I just don't think... I fit in." Wait, that was a little too close to vulnerability. "Or whatever," they add.

"Sure you do. The group needs a singer like you, and everyone likes you a lot. Basil couldn't stop talking about you last practice." Wesley tosses the paper into the small wastebasket under his desk. "And, for what it's worth, I really enjoy singing with you. Even if you are lip-syncing half the time."

Wesley looks at him, an easy smile spread across his face. His eyes sparkle even under these slightly flickering fluorescent lights. They're a nice dark brown, but when the light hits them just right, the inner rings around his pupils glow amber.

Quinn finds themself smiling back at him but drops it from their face as soon as they notice. "I'll come back for one more practice."

"That's great!"

"One."

"Then you only get one more tutoring session until you come to more practices."

"Ugh. Fine," Quinn mutters.

The next A Cademia practice is a day later. Quinn trudges into Theater B again.

"Quinn!" Basil exclaims and runs over. "I thought you weren't coming back!"

"Yeah, me neither. This guy drives a hard bargain, though," Quinn says, gesturing to Wesley who laughs. His eyes sparkle again.

Dove and Eddie are facing each other on the stage doing very intense vocal drills together, Eddie's countertenor voice mixing beautifully with Dove's soprano. Basil hops up on stage with them and adds her sweet alto to the mix.

"Come on," Wesley says.

Quinn barely has time to drop their backpack in a chair before Wesley puts his arm around their shoulders, guiding them up onto the stage. Wesley adds his rich, deep sound, and hesitantly, Quinn joins in with their shaky tenor voice. Carina adds some funky percussion.

They're just singing random chord progressions, but it sounds familiar. It sounds like… No way.

Quinn starts singing the lyrics to Mariah Carey's "All I Want for Christmas is You" and it fits surprisingly well with the chords they were already singing. The others' faces light up and they sing the song more purposefully, Dove joining in on the lyrics, singing high harmonies. They get to the second verse and Quinn has no idea what the words are, so the song devolves into laughter.

Wesley pats them on the shoulder. "That was great," he says with a smile.

Maybe this singing thing isn't so bad.

The rest of practice goes well, mostly vocal exercises and debating about what songs to choose for sectionals, which is coming up in a couple months or so.

"No more Journey," Dove says. "It was over with Glee. It's gotta be a Beyoncé medley."

"Medleys were over with Pitch Perfect," Carina says.

"You take that back," Dove says dangerously. "You take that shit back."

"Why don't we each pick a song or a medley and bring it for next week's practice? We'll vote and decide once and for all," Wesley suggests, and the others nod.

Two hours went by faster than ever now that Quinn actually let themself have a little fun. They sling one strap of their backpack over their shoulder and head for the door. Wesley catches up with them and they walk together to the library.

"What'd you think? You seemed a little more... engaged this time," Wesley says.

"Yeah, I dunno," Quinn says, looking down at their feet as they walk along the paved path through the green. "I did like it better this time. Maybe Mariah, patron saint of Christmas, blessed this practice."

Wesley laughs, deep and crisp. "Maybe so."

Quinn grimaces and rubs at their neck. The muscle between their neck and shoulder gets tight all the time from sleeping wrong, stress, or even just an extra book in their backpack.

"You okay?" Wesley asks, gesturing to his own neck.

"Yeah, fine. Just—tight. Needs to crack or something."

"Hold on." Wesley touches Quinn's shoulder to still them, then steps behind them and places his hands firmly on Quinn's neck.

"What are you—"

Then Wesley moves his hands quickly, pressing and twisting just a bit, and relief spreads through Quinn's body. They let out a groan, then feel heat rise to their cheeks.

Wesley's hands linger on Quinn for just a moment too long, so Quinn steps away and turns.

"Thanks."

"No problem."

Quinn's sure they're imagining the way Wesley's pupils are blown. It must be a shadow.

They reach the library and make their way to Wesley's desk where Quinn breaks the news.

"So…" they begin.

"Uh oh."

"The full research paper is due in a week."

"Yeah…?"

"And…" Quinn twists back and forth in their rolly chair.

"I don't like this," Wesley says.

"I wanna change my topic." Quinn braces themself for…

"You *what?*" That.

"I know, I know. Is that crazy?" Quinn asks.

Wesley spares no time in saying, "Yes!"

"Well, okay, so public transportation is so *blah*, and Professor Duke said it'd be okay if I changed my topic, and I want to choose one I actually care about."

"You're telling me you don't care about public transportation?" Wesley jokes.

"Not particularly," Quinn says with a lopsided smile.

"Well, where'd you get that topic from anyway?"

"She gave us a list of possible topics and I chose the first one."

"Okay, well, what do you wanna change to?"

Quinn smacks their forehead onto the desk. "I don't know."

Wesley takes a deep breath. Quinn half expects him to tell them they're an idiot, but instead, he says, "Well, let's start brainstorming."

In the end, they decide on the topic of music therapy. Quinn felt a spark of excitement the second Wesley mentioned it, and they knew it was the one.

Now to actually write the thing.

CHAPTER 7
PRESENT

"Okay, so what song?" Basil asks as they walk back to the house.

"We could do a—" Dove starts.

"Don't say medley," Eddie interrupts.

"Excuse me," Dove says with a playfully offended smile. "I was *going* to say we could do a mashup. That's different."

"Is it?" Eddie questions.

"Yes!" Dove smacks him hard on the arm.

"Mashups *do* usually do well at these sorts of things," Wesley points out. He pulls the key out of his pocket and unlocks the door to let them all in.

"A mashup of what, though?" Carina asks, tumbling over the back of the couch and landing on the cushions.

"Um… Disney?" Basil suggests.

"What about queens of pop? Dolly, Cher, Gaga?" Dove suggests.

"Beyoncé and Jennifer Hudson need to be added to that list," Eddie says from the kitchen.

"Of course!" Dove agrees.

"Quinn, what do you think?" Basil asks.

If they're honest, Quinn isn't even sure they want to participate, but Basil seems so excited, and they aren't about to rain on her birthday parade. "I really don't know, guys. I guess we could go with a song we all already know? That'd be easiest."

The others nod. Wesley says, "That's a good strategy. How about 'Persephone'?"

What he's referring to is Quinn's favorite song by their favorite band: 'Persephone's Downfall' by Curse of the Rebellion. They haven't listened to that song in about four months.

"Why would you want to do that?" Quinn asks, harsher than they meant.

Wesley frowns at them.

"That's the song we did at sectionals," Quinn says, though they all know. "Why would you wanna do it again?"

"It's a good song," Wesley says. "With some tweaks, I think it could be perfect for this. It'd stand out." Wesley eyes Quinn curiously, and Quinn crosses their arms more firmly across their chest and looks away. "If you don't want to do it, that's okay," Wesley says.

"No, it's fine."

"What about 'Persephone' in the style of... the Beach Boys?" Basil suggests.

"What?" Dove laughs. "How would that even work?"

Basil sings a couple bars and Eddie snaps along. He sees where she's heading and joins in with a high harmony. Basil grins and faces him, and they start dancing as they sing in the middle of the kitchen.

Dove joins in with some doo-wop scatting in the background and Wesley adds in a Beach Boys-style bass line just as Carina adds in some percussion.

Quinn uncrosses their arms. This is pretty good. No, this is really good. With the mixture of dark, edgy lyrics and lighthearted doo-wop, they might actually have something here. "Holy shit... We could really win."

Dove breaks out of the song to correct them: "No, baby. We're *going* to win."

♪♪♪

They spend a couple hours finalizing their 60's beachy arrangement of a dark and moody emo song. It's mostly Wesley, Dove, and Eddie working out the parts while Basil, Carina, and Quinn relax on the couch. Basil has turned on HGTV and they're watching a rich, white couple pick one of three beautiful houses to buy. The husband wants a historical home in the heart of downtown while his wife wants a new-construction mansion in the countryside. Why did they get married?

"I don't know," the man on TV says. *"I don't love this closet."*

"Are you kidding?" Basil says. She notices Quinn looking at her and explains, "My dorm is about as big as that closet. Have some perspective, *Michael*," she says to the TV.

Carina eventually disappears into the bedroom, then heads out to the beach, and Basil joins her after the episode ends.

Some show comes on about a husband and wife who flip houses while blindfolded, and Quinn loses interest. They wander over to the bookshelf beside the sliding glass door and flip through one of the books.

Everything on this shelf is covered in dust. Quinn picks up a seashell and can see the perfectly clean circle under it.

They wonder how long it's been since someone paid any attention to these books and knickknacks. They must be lonely.

"Hey."

Quinn jumps and spins around, nearly dropping the shell. Oh, it's Wesley. "Hey."

"I just wanted to make sure you're cool with us doing that song? I know it's your favorite. I don't want this dumb arrangement to ruin it for you or anything," Wesley says with a laugh.

"No, it's fine." It's already ruined. Quinn places the shell back on the shelf and nudges it back into place.

"Really? You just seemed... I don't know. Weirded out by my suggestion."

Quinn turns away from the shelf and faces Wesley. "Why would you want to do that song?" they ask again.

Wesley repeats his answer from earlier: "It's a good song."

"There are a lot of good songs."

"I like this one."

"Why?"

"Because I do."

"*Why?*" Quinn presses.

"Because of you!" Wesley says a little too loudly. Dove and Eddie pause their singing at the kitchen counter but resume after a moment. "Because you showed it to me."

"Then wouldn't you want to just forget it?"

"No. Why—" Wesley's eyebrow flicks as if Quinn's words stung. "I listen to it all the time."

Quinn frowns. Wesley looks earnest, even a little sheepish. He looks at the shelf instead of Quinn.

"Really?" Quinn asks in a small voice.

Wesley nods. He changes the subject, pointing at a book on the shelf. "This one's good." It's *Lord of the Flies*.

"I know," Quinn says. "I read it."

Wesley looks at him with a bemused smile. "You did?"

Quinn glances at him and shrugs. "You told me to."

That statement hangs between them, carrying more weight than it seems.

Wesley gets a look on his face Quinn doesn't like. "Hey, listen, I'm really—"

"I'm going outside." Quinn opens the sliding door and steps out, shutting it behind them. They feel a little guilty for cutting Wesley off like that, but they knew what he was going to say, and they aren't ready to hear it.

Quinn walks down toward the shoreline and looks out at the ocean. It's low tide but the waves still reach Quinn's feet, sucking the sand beneath them out to sea. They sink slowly and imagine being sucked all the way under until they can barely see the sky.

A hand closes on their shoulder. It's Carina.

She pulls her large sunglasses off, Basil's floppy sun hat shading her face well enough. A red sarong is wrapped around her waist. "Hey, bud," she says.

"Hey," Quinn says as they turn back toward the ocean.

"Pretty," Carina says simply.

Quinn hums in agreement.

"You don't have to talk about how you're feeling, but you probably will have to face it one way or another."

Will they? They heave a sigh. "I don't know. I think if I can just get through this trip, I'll never have to see him again."

"Is that what you want, though?"

Truthfully? No.

Does Quinn wish they were still angry and hateful? Yes. That'd be easier than the alternative—full of questions, yet somehow empty. They don't hate Wesley anymore, if they ever did. And they aren't still sad or upset. They just feel...

unfinished. It feels like the whole situation never ended. "I think I want closure."

"Classic for movie breakups."

"No, but I really think I do. How do you get that?"

Quinn expects some life-changing piece of wisdom like usual, but instead, she shrugs. "Dunno. Never been broken up with."

Quinn looks at her. "Never?"

"I'm the dumper. Never the dumpee."

"Huh."

"Best I can guess is that you need to rehash it all. Get it out in the open. Then you can talk it through to a close."

"But I don't wanna do that."

Carina shrugs and slips her sunglasses back on. "Then don't."

She walks back to the house, leaving Quinn alone except for Basil snoozing on a beach towel ten yards away.

Getting closure sounds... uncomfortable. Quinn lets out a sigh. Maybe they don't need it. Maybe they can just suffer through this week without bringing up anything about the past. That still seems like the best way through.

Quinn has a feeling Wesley's going to make that difficult.

CHAPTER 8
PAST

Even Quinn is surprised when they continue attending practices. They were sure they wouldn't be back after Wesley made them do lip trills to the tune of the Hallelujah Chorus, buzzing their lips while humming a god-awful Christmas song with a thousand harmonies, all fully a cappella. It was simultaneously difficult and embarrassing.

But Quinn came back and was given a sweet greeting by Basil, who ran up to them and hugged them around the neck.

Now, the six of them are sitting in the chairs of the small black box theater talking about their sectionals setlist.

"It has to be shocking," Eddie says. "During my freshman year we did a Broadway medley. It killed, but the judges hated it. Said it had been done too many times."

"Aw, but a Broadway medley would be so fun!" Dove says. "What about… Wesley, do we still have sheet music for *Into the Woods?*"

"Too hard," Wesley says. "Remember when we tried before? Even Carter couldn't handle it." To Quinn, he explains, "Carter was the tenor then. He was the best in the club until he graduated."

"Big shoes to fill," Eddie says.

"Hey, what do you think we should sing, Quinn?" Basil asks.

Quinn smiles at her attempt to include them, but waves her off, saying, "Oh, no, I'm not experienced in this kind of thing. I don't know what judges are looking for."

"We do know, though, and it gives us analysis paralysis," Wesley says. "You choose."

"I can't, guys."

"Come on! What's your favorite song?" Dove asks.

Lyrics about Persephone killing Hades come to mind, but no. Their favorite music doesn't really mesh with the a cappella style. They're all about show tunes and pop song covers.

"Say it, Quinn," Carina commands.

"'Persephone's Downfall'," Quinn admits. "But it's weird emo stuff, you guys don't have to do it—"

"Here," Dove says, holding up her phone as the song starts to play. Energetic drums spill from her speakers and Carina nods along, tapping on her thigh. The vocals come in with some powerful screaming and Dove bobs her head in time with it.

"This is good," Eddie says, listening intently.

"Good choice, Quinn!" Basil says.

Quinn feels the tension in their chest start to release. Their music taste is really personal to them. They wouldn't be able to handle any ridicule, so it's nice that they're accepting it even though it's probably very different from what they usually sing and listen to.

"This could work," Wesley says seriously. Quinn can see him working out the arrangement in his mind. He looks up. "Yeah, this could really work."

Wesley pulls up the song on his own phone and sits down at the piano on the far left of the room. He jots down notes in his notebook, playing certain chords and finding progressions that work. Dove stands beside him helping and making suggestions here and there. Quinn will admit, they haven't seen someone their age so dedicated to their craft. It's kind of inspiring.

…Dumb craft, though. Not that inspiring.

After around twenty minutes, Wesley has come up with a nearly complete arrangement of 'Persephone's Downfall', and he and Dove sing it for the group while he plays the missing notes on the piano. After he's finished, he turns around on the bench and looks directly at Quinn. "Well?"

It takes a beat for them to realize he's nervous about Quinn's reaction. "Oh, um, yeah. It was good."

"Did you like it?"

"It actually suits the song really well, um…" Quinn gets up and walks over to point at Wesley's notebook still open on the piano. "I really liked this part—here. Where the higher part is kind of—uh, what's the word? When the notes don't sound quite right?"

"Dissonant?"

"Yeah. Dissonant with the lower part. It's kind of symbolic, you know? It fits the lyrics really well."

Wesley smiles at him, wide and bright. "I'm glad you think so. Would it be cool with you if we sang this at sectionals?"

Quinn smiles and says, "Of course. It'd be awesome."

Wesley reaches up and squeezes Quinn's elbow. They smile at each other for a moment too long. Quinn coughs and looks away.

The rest of the group comes closer to see the rough sheet music Wesley wrote down.

"Who's the soloist?" Basil asks.

Wesley says, "I'm not sure. It could suit a few different voice parts, honestly." An odd look crosses his face. "Quinn, you should do it."

"Yeah!" Dove agrees.

"What?" Quinn's eyes widen.

"It's your favorite song!" Basil exclaims.

"Yeah, and the melody line would definitely work for tenor. That'd be perfect!" Eddie says.

"Oh, um, no, I think someone more experienced should do it," Quinn says.

"No way, Quinn. This is your song," Basil says.

Preemptive stage fright bubbles up in Quinn's throat. They haven't sung in front of anyone but these five losers, and they expect them to sing lead on this song during a competition? Quinn shakes their head. "No, I can't."

Wesley senses their very real fear and says, "I'll sing it with you."

"Really?"

"Of course. I can rework it as a duet."

Quinn nods. "Okay. If it's a duet... I think I could maybe do that."

Wesley smiles at them and makes a note on the page: *quinn/wesley duet*. Something about that gives Quinn butterflies, but it isn't stage fright.

CHAPTER 9
PRESENT

Quinn's alarm goes off at 6 AM, and they join the others, minus Basil, in the living room. Four of them put up a banner, streamers, and balloons while Carina makes pancakes. A bright blue cake sits on the counter with blue candles. Unfortunately, they couldn't find candles that burn blue. They looked, too.

Around 7 AM, Basil emerges from her room, saying, "What are you guys doing up—*What!*" She looks around the living room with her hands on her cheeks. "You guys did all this for me? And it's all blue, look!"

The balloons and streamers are all turquoise, and the banner that says *HAPPY BDAY BAS!* is blue too.

"Order up," Carina says, handing Basil a plate of blue pancakes.

Basil nearly screams. "You guys!"

It's Basil's birthday, but it's also the day before the 6th Annual Conch Republic Music Jamboree, so the six of them are sitting on beach towels by the water practicing their song. All their voices are meshing, their pitches are perfect, and they've got the rhythms down.

But it sucks.

Quinn doesn't want to say anything because yeah, they may be moody most of the time but they don't actually want to be an asshole. It's true though—something just isn't working. Quinn is dutifully singing the part they were given, but one look at Wesley tells them that he agrees.

After one more run-through, Wesley finally stops them. "Something's off."

Immediately, the others agree.

"Oh my god, I *know*," Dove says, fanning herself with her sheet music.

"Is it me? You guys would tell me if it was me, right?" Eddie asks.

"Guys..." Basil says. "I think it might be... the soloists."

"But you're a soloist," Dove says. It's true—Basil and Eddie were singing lead.

"I know," Basil nods solemnly. "But I think we all know that's what's off." She looks pointedly at Wesley, and he looks away.

Quinn frowns. What could she mean? Wesley glances up at Quinn, and suddenly they understand. "No." Quinn is not singing the duet with Wesley. It's simply not happening.

"But Quinn—" Basil starts.

"No. I'm not singing with him."

"Just try it? Please?" Basil says, and Quinn would swear she's pouting her bottom lip out.

It *is* her birthday, and this *is* for the good of the group. "Fine. We can—" The group cheers and Quinn finishes, "We can try it. For now."

Wesley plays everyone's starting notes on his piano app. Quinn and Wesley sing the melody lines one octave lower than Basil and Eddie were singing them, so it's easy to adjust their notes to theirs. Carina begins the percussion, Eddie tries his best at singing Wesley's bass line, and the others form the doo-wop background for Wesley and Quinn.

Quinn admits to themself that the song is working now. This is what it needed.

They reach the point of dissonance, when their notes don't match up all the way, just as Persephone is expressing her conflicted feelings about Hades in the song. Quinn glances up at Wesley over their sheet music and—

No.

A quick jolt of warmth spreads through Quinn's stomach and they look away, fixing their eyes on a bird running along the edge of the water.

That wasn't a spark. It wasn't.

Wesley had looked at them, eyes gleaming and a smile tucked in the corner of his mouth. He looked at them like—

Like before.

No way.

The group finishes the song, makes some tweaks, and when they feel it's where it needs to be, they head back to the house for lunch.

Carina made everyone ham and cheese sandwiches, and Dove gives her a kiss on the cheek when she sees Carina made hers with vegan lunch meat and imitation cheese. Quinn doesn't miss the way Carina's cheeks redden. When she notices them looking, she shoots them a glare that guarantees Quinn won't breathe a word of it to anyone.

Quinn grabs their sandwich and sits on the couch. They discover it reclines, so they pull the handle, and the footrest kicks out. Basil turns the TV back on and flips through the channels.

"Ghostly Love 6!" Eddie exclaims.

"What's Ghostly Love?" Basil asks.

"Only the best horror-romance film franchise in the world," he replies.

"Beg to differ," Dove says. "*Haunted* Love is better."

"That's a freaking spin-off of Ghostly Love. Spin-offs are always chasing the success of the original."

"The romance is just better in Ghostly Love," Dove says.

"Or maybe romance doesn't belong in horror at all," Quinn says around a mouthful of ham and cheese.

"Maybe you should shut your mouth." Dove shoots a glare their way.

The group ends up watching a different movie altogether. This one is about dinosaurs. They reach the end and as the meteor is plummeting toward Earth, Eddie and Dove are holding each other, tears in their eyes. The screen fades to black and credits roll.

"What the hell?" Eddie says, wiping his eyes. "They spent 90 minutes making us care about two triceratopses and then they just kill them like that?"

"Not cool," Dove agrees. "Why would they kill them at the end?"

"Um... You guys know that that's actually what happened, right?" Wesley asks carefully.

Dove throws her crumpled up napkin at him. "Not helping!"

When some cheesy romcom comes on, everyone wanders away, leaving Quinn on the couch and Wesley in one of the chairs. Quinn wills him not to say anything.

It doesn't work.

"We sounded good, I think."

Quinn nods.

"It's crazy because it's been so long since we sang together. Same song, too."

Quinn nods again, still not meeting Wesley's eyes.

"Are you—How do you feel? About the duet?"

Quinn risks a glance and sees... insecurity? "Fine," they answer simply.

A silence settles between them. Quinn can sense Wesley trying to find something to say, so they save him the trouble.

"Look, we sounded good tonight. And we'll sound good tomorrow at the Jamboree thing or whatever. But that doesn't mean things are back to how they were. Things can stay how they are now. You don't talk to me, I don't talk to you, and that's it."

Wesley's face crumples. "You don't mean that, right? We'll just never talk?"

"Why would you *want* to talk to me? The last things you said to me at school made it pretty clear you'd never want anything to do with me."

"I'm sorry about that, Quinn. I've said I'm sorry. I texted you every day for weeks, just saying sorry."

Quinn crosses their arms tighter and looks away. Out of the corner of their eye, they see Wesley reach his hand out toward them, then fold it back in his lap.

Quinn trusted this person once. Maybe even loved him. Look how that turned out. They aren't making that mistake twice.

They walk into their room, hoping Wesley doesn't follow.

"Hey man!" Eddie greets them when they walk in. He's lying on his back on the far-right bed with his arms and legs hanging off at odd angles.

"Hey. You okay?" Quinn asks, eyeing his odd position.

"I'm about to take a nap and Carina told me I can astral project if I sleep like this."

"Carina told you that, huh?"

Eddie nods. Classic Carina. Making Eddie look like an idiot even when she's not around to see the fruits of her labor. A selfless woman.

Quinn collapses on their own bed in the center and stares up at the rough-textured, water-damaged ceiling. There are cobwebs in the upper corners of the room, and one blows around from the air of the ceiling fan.

This is impossible.

Quinn is here for Basil and their other friends only, but Wesley seems like he's trying to reconnect. Why would he do that? After what went down between them four months ago, after what was said, Quinn wouldn't have ever thought Wesley would stand to see them again, let alone speak to them.

And now they're singing together.

Quinn covers their face with the pillow and groans.

"Hey, keep it down," Eddie says. "Thanks. Now I have to start all over."

"You're not gonna astral project, Edward."

"Not with that attitude."

Not with that attitude. Maybe Quinn just needs to adjust how they're looking at the situation. They already established they want closure. That's not going to happen if they keep trying to avoid Wesley.

But Quinn *really* wants to avoid him.

CHAPTER 10
PAST

Quinn's research paper is actually going well.

Wesley made them a writing schedule and they've been sticking to it, surprisingly enough. It has nothing to do with the pride on Wesley's face every time Quinn tells him they worked on it.

Okay, maybe it has something to do with that. Whenever Quinn shows an ounce of promise, Wesley grins this beautiful grin, wide and toothy, like he means it. Maybe he does mean it. But Quinn is certain he acts this way with all his tutoring students.

Right?

Quinn looks over at Wesley who's watching their screen intently as Quinn scrolls through what they have so far. Wesley looks over when the screen stills.

"How many people do you tutor?"

"What?" Wesley asks with a laugh, confused.

"Like… it's not just me, right?"

Wesley fixes them with an amused look, a slight smile playing at the corners of his mouth. "Would it be so bad if it were?"

Quinn meets his eyes.

"Maybe you're special," Wesley says quietly.

They stare at each other for a few beats before Wesley turns back to the research paper like nothing had happened.

"I like what you have so far. I would say switch these two paragraphs and develop this idea a little more. Oh, and you didn't cite this quote anywhere."

Quinn frowns at him. "Okay."

"It's about that time. I'll walk you out."

Wesley stands while Quinn packs up their notebook and thumb drive. Together, they walk out of the library.

It's a beautiful day and Quinn shades their eyes to look at the puffy clouds. They're probably dark storm clouds for the town over, but to Quinn, they look pure white.

"Hey, um," Wesley begins. He sounds uncharacteristically nervous, and Quinn looks over with a frown. "I don't know if you'd be interested, like, at all, but…" *'Like'?* A filler word? He really must be nervous. "I was wondering if you'd ever want to go get dinner or something? Or lunch. Or coffee. It's really up to you. If you even want to, of course. I mean—"

"Sure," Quinn says, saving him from his rambling.

Wesley looks at him for a moment before saying, "It's as a date."

"…I know." For a smart guy, he's pretty dumb.

"I just wanted to make sure you understood."

Quinn laughs. "I do. When do you want to go?"

"Up to you. You can look at your calendar and decide then."

"You think I have a calendar?"

Wesley looks offended. "How do you ever know what you're doing that day?"

Quinn grins. "I don't."

Wesley is about to argue, then lets out a breath laughs. "Well, I'll see you then."

"I'll text you," Quinn says.

"Yeah." Wesley rubs the back of his neck. "Okay, um…"
He punches Quinn lightly on the shoulder.

"What was that?"

"I don't know!"

This is going to be an awkward date.

♪♪♪

It is.

A few days later, they meet at a cafe downtown around lunchtime. It's a nice place with lots of natural light, unique, mismatched chairs at every table, and local art on the walls. Quinn can't honestly say the local art is any good, but it does add to the ambience.

Quinn arrives first and sits down at a two-person table toward the back beside a bookcase full of old books.

After a few minutes, Wesley walks in. He takes his sunglasses off and orders something at the counter, then looks around. His face brightens when he spots them.

"Hey," Wesley says, pulling out the empty chair.

Quinn sits up straighter. "Hey."

"How's it going?"

"Good." There's a second of awkward silence so Quinn asks, "What'd you order?"

"Americano."

"Ew, really?" Quinn jokes, wrinkling their nose.

"Yeah. They're good," Wesley replies seriously.

"Oh, I was just... Uh, so how are you today?"

"I'm doing well. I went to the gym earlier."

"Oh yeah? What'd you do?"

The whole time Wesley answers, Quinn internally panics about the awkwardness. They thought this would be pretty normal. They get along fine during tutoring and a cappella practice, and it's never awkward like this. If the date continues this way, they might not be able to face him again. There goes their English score. No way are they going to turn in a good research paper without him. *Just keep smiling and nodding.*

A barista approaches with both their drinks in novelty mugs and sits them down in front of them. Quinn has a cow print mug with four pink rubber feet... udders. Wesley has a smaller mug shaped like a carrot.

Quinn smiles at the barista. "Thank you," *for saving me.* They take a sip. "Wow, that's really good. How's yours?"

Wesley is still blowing into his mug. "Too hot still. Haven't tried it."

Quinn nods. This is going nowhere. They reach for the sugar canister sitting on the table and their arm brushes their cup. Apparently, udders aren't a stable base for a mug, because it tumbles off and smashes on the floor, light brown liquid going everywhere, mixing in with cow print shards.

Wesley lets out a loud snort, then covers his mouth.

They make eye contact, and neither can stifle their giggles. Quinn wheezes silently until they can't breathe, and Wesley covers his mouth, but his watering eyes give him away.

A barista comes over with rags and a broom and Quinn cleans up their mess.

The curse is broken. After that, things are back to normal, and their banter freely flows.

After chatting for a while about anything and everything, Wesley points at the bookcase behind Quinn. "Hey, Lord of the Flies."

Quinn turns and hums. "What about it?"

"Isn't that one of the books you didn't read in English?"

Quinn laughs. "Yes, one of many. Good memory."

"You really should give it a read."

"Why though? Isn't it just about a bunch of boys on an island killing pigs?"

"No, it's—actually, that *is* a pretty good synopsis. But the symbolism and meaning go way deeper than that. It's worth reading if you ever have time."

Quinn takes a sip of their replacement drink and nods.

They keep talking and laughing until Quinn glances at their phone and sees it's been two hours. They point this out to Wesley, who says he has a class he needs to get ready for, so they walk out together.

"I'd like to see you again," Wesley says.

"You see me every Tuesday."

"You know what I mean."

Quinn smiles softly. "I do."

"See you, Quinn."

"Smell ya later."

When Quinn arrives back at their dorm, they can't help but let out a squeal. They don't think they've ever made that noise before, but then again, they don't think they've ever met a guy like Wesley before, either.

CHAPTER 11
PRESENT

"Part of Miss Basil's Tropical Birthday Extravaganza," Dove announces, "is a kayak tour! Suit up in your swimsuits and meet me at the front door in ten."

Everyone jumps up and heads into the rooms to change. Once again, Quinn changes into their suit in the bathroom.

They do their best to fix their messy mop of hair in the mirror, then head to the front door, and the group embarks on their journey.

Their Uber minivan drops them off at the mouth of a canal where a man in a safari hat and a psychedelic wolf t-shirt is waiting for them with seven brightly colored kayaks prepared to launch.

"Greetings, voyagers," the man yells. "My name is Captain Mike. I will be your guide for today." A flock of birds flies out of the nearby mangroves.

They introduce themselves to Captain Mike and he hands each of them a life jacket, a dry-box for their phones, and a paddle. He demonstrates how to use it to turn, stop, and accelerate.

Once Captain Mike deems them ready to set sail, he helps each of them climb into their kayaks. Quinn goes last which is probably a mistake because now all their friends are ready and waiting while Quinn stares at the bright orange boat in fear.

Captain Mike stands with one foot on the kayak, holding it steady for Quinn. He holds out a sweaty hand, but Quinn opts to lean down with both hands braced on the sides of the tiny boat.

"It's best to just sit quickly," Captain Mike says, but Quinn has already committed to crawling.

They take tiny steps on their hands and knees until they are firmly on the kayak. It rocks dangerously beneath them, and they shift their weight to keep their balance, but they overcompensate and now the boat is rocking even worse.

"Now sit—No, just—" Captain Mike tries to help them but has obviously never seen this approach before.

Quinn finally sits down in the kayak and it levels out. That went pretty well. They only teared up a little.

Captain Mike hands them their paddle and Quinn is off to the races. Captain Mike easily gets onto his own kayak and the group heads off through the narrow canal.

It's about eight feet wide and covered by an arch of gnarled mangrove branches. A small white bird with a long neck and long legs hides within the tangle of roots. Sunlight filters in and shimmers on the water as their kayaks gently bob on the calm current.

Captain Mike guides them through this leg of the canal and soon they leave the mangroves, suddenly in a wider section with nothing but a few clouds overhead. Quinn wishes they had put on sunscreen.

Dove's kayak catches up and bumps Quinn's and they smack the nose of her boat with their paddle. She laughs and reaches into the water to splash them. Quinn shoots her a death glare.

They continue paddling at a lazy pace until they end up in a very wide river with larger boats passing by. They send waves out in their wake that rock the kayaks and make Quinn clutch at their life jacket.

"We're gonna turn left and continue on this leg of the river," Captain Mike announces. He's around 30 feet away but Quinn heard him just fine, even over the motors of nearby boats. Now Quinn understands why he's so loud.

They follow his lead and soon they're back in a quiet and calm strip of water. There are a few large houses with private piers reaching out towards them, and Basil narrowly avoids drifting into one.

Quinn's shoulders start to sting, and they glance down and see they're already turning red. "Carina, do you have the sunscreen?"

Carina looks back and nods. She reaches down into her kayak and pulls out the yellow tube.

Quinn paddles closer and takes it from her. She continues on with the rest of the group.

They rest their paddle across their kayak and open the tube, squeezing out a liberal amount. They coat their shoulders in it, ignoring the raw feeling as they rub their hands over the fresh sunburns. They go ahead and do their knees too since their legs are facing the sun and are sure to burn soon as well.

As Quinn moves their leg to get a better angle, they bump their paddle and it slips. They move lightning-fast to catch it, but their fingers hit it instead of grab it, and the paddle tumbles into the water. It floats, and Quinn tries to snatch it back up, but their sudden movement starts to tip their kayak—not capsizing them, but nearly.

The current carries their paddle toward the mangrove roots, and it lodges itself there a few yards ahead. Quinn's kayak is slowly carried toward their friends by the current, but by now, they're too far away to hear them when they shout, "Guys! Guys, I'm stuck!"

Quinn knows they'll realize soon, and they won't die out here, but a vulture circling overhead seems to think otherwise.

At least they have sunscreen.

They watch as their friends get further and further away, shrinking into the distance. Quinn grabs onto a barnacle-covered post of a pier and stills their kayak in the shade. The group turns around a corner. They'll come back soon, but the wait is gonna suck.

After a few minutes, a kayak appears again, coming towards them. It's probably Captain Mike, who sees a lawsuit in his future.

As the kayaker gets closer, Quinn can make out dark skin and bright salmon-colored swim trunks. Not Captain Mike.

Wesley.

Finally he gets within earshot and Wesley calls, "What happened?"

"I lost my paddle," Quinn replies. "It's over..." They point to the mangrove roots, but the paddle is nowhere to be seen.

"Grab onto my kayak," Wesley says, closer now and turning so Quinn faces his back. Quinn reaches forward, but the nose of the kayak is too long, and they can't reach it.

They tell Wesley as much, and Wesley backs up until he's next to them and has them grab the side. When Wesley starts trying to paddle, they realize the flaw in that plan.

Quinn shrieks as the paddle nearly smacks them in the face.

Wesley pulls his mouth to one side in thought. Then a grimace crosses his face. "We could... Well..."

"What?"

Wesley fixes them with a look that says, 'I don't like this any more than you do.' He sighs and says, "You can get on my kayak."

"How about—Okay, I'll go next to you but I'll hold further back. Then you won't hit me in the face."

They try it, Quinn on Wesley's right, but as soon as Wesley moves forward, physics gets in their way. Quinn's kayak begins to point to the right, and it's not long before they drift apart and Quinn can't hold on anymore.

Quinn glares at Wesley. "Fine."

"Hey, it's not my favorite idea either, but it's all I can think of that would work. Unless you want to get out and walk."

Quinn does not. "Okay, how do we do this?"

Wesley thinks for a moment. "Okay, see those stairs on the other side of the pier? Use those to climb out of your kayak. Then I'll move mine up next to you and you can climb in from there." Quinn notices the second seat in the front of Wesley's kayak as he grabs the seatback and lifts it upright, pulling the straps on the sides to secure it in that position.

The plan goes well, except for Wesley's steadying hands on Quinn's waist. They're big and warm and distracting and—

They smack them off and settle into the seat.

"Now we ride like the wind," Wesley says stupidly because he's a dumb moron.

It's not... bad. Quinn doesn't mind relaxing, not having to do anything but float. But Wesley being right behind them, breathing heavily from paddling, undoubtedly looking like the Greek god of kayaking, is not great for Quinn's plan of avoiding him.

All of this leaves Quinn's mind the second they see the fin lift from the water. "Oh my god, is that a shark?" They point to where the fin had surfaced.

"Where? I don't see anything."

Quinn's eyes dart around near where they had seen it. A sliver pokes up again. "There!"

"Where?"

"It was right there! Oh my god, we're gonna get eaten!" Quinn grips their life jacket tightly.

"I'll beat it away with the paddle."

"The paddle!" Quinn says, remembering a tweet they'd seen about surfers looking like seals. "It probably sees the shape of us with the paddle and thinks we're a seal."

"I don't think there are seals in the Keys."

"Oh god, then it's really hungry!"

Wesley laughs behind them.

"What the hell is funny?"

"You," Wesley answers simply.

Quinn is about to retort when they see it again. "There! You had to have seen it that time!"

Wesley laughs again, louder and longer. "Yes, I did."

"Why are you laughing? It's a *shark!*"

The fin surfaces again, this time closer, and Quinn screams.

Wesley laughs again and grips Quinn's shoulder. "Relax," he says quietly. "It's just a dolphin."

"It—what?" Quinn watches it surface one more time and this time, they see its blowhole. "Oh."

Wesley chuckles. They watch the dolphin play in the water for a while longer.

"Isn't it beautiful?" Wesley says.

"Yeah," Quinn agrees. They watch as the dolphin dashes through the water, surfacing in a different spot each time. The sun glistens on its slick, gray back. There must be a lot of fish, because it's still dancing through the water even after they pass.

They continue on and eventually meet back up with the group who has stopped and is receiving a lecture from Captain Mike about types of barnacles.

"Quinn!" Basil greets them.

"You guys waited for me?"

"Of course," Dove says. "When Wes realized you weren't with us, we stopped right away."

Wesley is the one who realized they were missing? Quinn doesn't know how they feel about that. They almost feel flattered. Yuck.

The group continues the tour, but Wesley and Quinn hang back a bit. They can still hear Captain Mike, of course. It would be impossible not to.

"Quinn, I know you've been avoiding me this week and I—"

"No—"

"And I understand why," Wesley finishes. "The things I said and did weren't okay. I'm sorry." Wesley lets out a bitter laugh. "I've been trying to say that to you all week."

"Thanks."

Wesley doesn't reply.

They end up back in a narrow corridor of mangroves and Wesley says, "This would be such a nice picture."

Quinn bristles. "Mm-hm."

"Hey, do you still do film photography?"

"No," Quinn replies coldly.

"Oh." Wesley doesn't ask any other questions.

They pull up to where they had launched, and Captain Mike helps everyone get out of their kayaks.

"Sorry I left mine," Quinn says.

"Eh, happens all the time. Usually someone flips over. Least ya didn't do that."

They thank Captain Mike, and he climbs back into his kayak to go get the one Quinn had abandoned.

"Quinn—" Wesley begins.

"Thank you for coming back for me. That was nice of you. But we really don't have to talk."

Quinn hazards a glance at Wesley's face and sees dejection. They feel bad for a moment before remembering Wesley's photography comment. How dare he bring that up so casually? Doesn't he remember what he did?

That's why Quinn doesn't want to talk to this guy. Quinn doesn't want to just gloss over everything that happened. It seems like Wesley just wants to forget about it all.

Quinn has a hard time forgetting.

CHAPTER 12
PAST

Quinn wakes up happy for the first time in a while.

The sun streams into their dorm and their roommate is still out somewhere, so they have the place to themself.

Quinn sits up and stretches, then grabs their phone. They have a text from Wesley: *See you soon!*

They shoot back a heart emoji.

They and Wesley have been on a few more dates, and each went much better than the first. One was to a retro arcade where Quinn obliterated Wesley at ski ball, and another was to some historical play at the university. The English department offered extra credit to anyone who went. The play sucked, but they got to laugh about it together, and that's all that matters. Plus Quinn's extra five points.

They've thrown themself further into their hobby and have started bringing their film camera everywhere. It's even earned them a nickname from their friends: Canon, for the brand of the camera. It's nice to have a nickname.

Quinn gets dressed, deliberating over which black graphic tee to wear before finally deciding on one that looks more or less exactly like the rest of them. But it has to be perfect. They're going on a picnic with Wesley today.

They grab their camera and loop the strap over their head, then set out to where they agreed to meet.

Quinn sits on the bench outside of the library watching birds in the nearby tree. They have a nest, and Quinn can just barely see it from their angle. They lift their camera from where it hangs around their neck and snap a picture. They're excited to see how that photo develops once this roll of film is finished.

Finally, Wesley appears. He's wearing a blue and white striped tank top with shorts that show off his toned shoulders, and Quinn has never been so attracted to someone holding a frilly picnic basket in one hand. Wesley reaches the other hand out and Quinn takes it, standing from the bench. They walk through the green together until they pick a tree to sit beneath. It's shady and doesn't have an ant hill at the base, so this won't be a repeat of their third date. Perfect.

Wesley lays out a blanket and sets the basket on one corner to weigh it down. He and Quinn sit, and he hands Quinn a sandwich in a baggie.

"Thanks." Quinn smiles at him.

It's a beautiful day to be done with a research paper. That's why Wesley planned this picnic—to celebrate Quinn's achievement. Quinn figures it wouldn't be a big deal for Wesley himself to finish a paper, but they're glad he recognizes how huge this is for Quinn.

The clouds are lit in such a way that Quinn decides they need to take a photo. They advance the film to prepare for the shot, then squeeze the shutter button to check the settings. Happy with how the shot will come out, they squeeze the button the rest of the way and hear a satisfying click as the camera immortalizes the blue sky.

Wesley takes a bite of his sandwich. "How did you learn to use that?" he asks.

"You're gonna laugh at me."

"Why?"

"YouTube," Quinn admits.

"Why would I laugh at that?"

"It'd be cooler to say my grandpa taught me while we were hiking the Appalachian Trail, but I learned to use a piece of analog technology through the internet. Kinda dumb."

"Nah. However you learn is valid. I bet 90 percent of the people at this school wouldn't even know where to start with that thing."

Quinn smiles. "It's easy. I'll show you."

They teach Wesley the key parts of the camera, and Wesley asks questions at all the right spots to make Quinn feel sufficiently interesting.

"You really learned all this online?" Wesley asks.

Quinn nods. "There's a super helpful channel called 'Rick's Gadgets' and he talks about all kinds of things. He even showed how to—" Quin stops themselves. "Sorry."

"For what?"

"Talking your ear off." Quinn laughs joylessly, then looks up when Wesley places a hand on their shoulder.

"Hey. I like you," Wesley says. "I like to talk to you. I like when you talk to me. You don't have to apologize for doing something I like."

The corner of Quinn's mouth flicks up without their permission. "I could love you," they blurt. Their eyes go wide, but they're saved from panicking by Wesley's enormous grin.

"I could love you too, Canon."

They stare at each other for just a moment, Quinn in disbelief that any of that just happened, and Wesley apparently over the moon judging by the way his eyes have disappeared into his smile.

"Let's take some of us," Wesley finally says.

"Pictures?"

"Yeah."

"A selfie on a film camera?"

"Why not?"

Quinn turns the camera around to face the two of them. They grab Wesley by the chin and turn his face to kiss him. Just as their lips touch, the shutter clicks and Quinn looks back at the camera, advancing the film.

Wesley brings his own hands up to Quinn's cheeks and kisses them again. Quinn takes another photo.

They eat together in comfortable silence, Quinn snapping more pictures of the blue sky, of people playing hack sack, of Wesley as he leans back against the tree with his eyes closed. Quinn can tell that's going to be one of their favorite pictures they've ever taken.

♪♫♪

The next time they meet up, they go bowling.

Quinn is a master bowler. They hold the ball, fingers in the holes, the other bracing it, and they raise it to their chest and let out a breath. Then they take one, two, three, four steps before releasing the ball. It sails down the alley toward the last three pins left standing. There are no survivors.

Quinn turns back around, triumphant fists in the air as Wesley smiles at them. Their phone buzzes in their pocket, and when they glance at the screen, they see a notification from the university's grade app.

"Wesley, Duke graded it!"

"Your paper?"

"Yeah!" Quinn opens the grades tab and sees... "76!"

"What?"

"I got a 76 percent!" Quinn feels even better than when they got a strike a few minutes ago.

"But you worked so hard."

"I know!"

"You only got a C?"

Quinn's smile falls. "What do you mean?"

"We worked so hard, and you barely passed? That's ridiculous."

"No, this is good, Wes. This is the highest I've gotten on a paper. Aren't you... proud of me?"

As they say this, the bowling alley's lights dim and technicolor strobe lights come on as loud music plays. Quinn wonders if Wesley heard them over it. Someone announces it's time for cosmic bowling.

Wesley did hear them. His scowl softens and he stands up. "Of course I'm proud of you." He wraps his arms around Quinn. "I'm sorry. I was just surprised. It deserved an A in my opinion."

Quinn smiles, but they're not sure if they mean it. How could he act like Quinn's achievement is a failure? They brush it off. He couldn't have meant it that way. "Thanks. Your turn."

CHAPTER 13
PRESENT

Apparently, kayaking works up an appetite. They end up at a seafood place in the center of town. It's beach-themed like just about everything else here, and Quinn normally wouldn't be caught dead in a restaurant that makes their female servers dress in tiny sailor outfits, but Basil had her heart set on coconut shrimp for dinner, and this was the only place on Yelp with a decent rating and fewer than three dollar signs.

Quinn isn't a fan of seafood, but they power through for Basil, who is clearly enjoying her shrimp by the way she's dancing in her seat.

"So, Carina, Wesley, and Eddie," Dove begins. "You three graduated last semester. What have you been up to since?"

Carina answers first. "I'm nannying."

Everyone at the table is surprised.

"Nannying?" Dove repeats, and Carina nods. "I had no idea you like kids."

"Don't," Carina responds. "Makes me great at controlling them, though. I don't even come close to giving in to their demands."

"Demands? How old are they?" Quinn asks, picturing unruly teens.

"Two and four."

"My niece and nephew are two and four, too!" Basil says. "Aren't they so cute at that age?"

Carina grips her margarita. "The cutest."

"So Eddie, what about you?" Dove asks.

Eddie is still wearing his sunglasses because he forgot his regular glasses at the house. He looks cooler than he has any right to be. "I've been doing this and that. A little here, a little there."

"So... unemployed," Wesley says.

Eddie sticks a finger in the air. "Actually, I am incredibly employed by a lot of different people at different times. So. The opposite of unemployed. Thanks." He smiles sarcastically and tosses a popcorn shrimp into his mouth.

"What kind of work are you doing?" Quinn asks.

"All kinds. I did construction for this one mansion. I was a poolboy for a hot minute. Oh, oh, I ran the puppet show for this library for a few weeks. I had to stop when they started getting complaints of it being too graphic." Eddie scoffs. "If they want a fairytale puppet show about slaying a dragon that *doesn't* include realistic gore, they're in for an unpleasant surprise when they find out all puppeteers share my preferences for visceral storytelling."

Dove wrinkles her face and stares at him. "What was any of that?"

"Musings of an *employed* man." Eddie shoots a look at Wesley.

Dove changes the subject. "Wesley, what about you?"

"I've been doing some tutoring online here and there."

Quinn slides a chunk of their fish around on their plate. Why is he tutoring again if he hated it so much?

"Nice!" Basil says. "A lot of students?"

"Some."

"Got a favorite?" she asks.

Quinn doesn't miss the way Wesley glances at them for a fraction of a second. "There's a little girl from Beijing who's really eager to learn and gets mad every time the timer goes off at the end of the lesson." He laughs. "She's a cutie."

"Sounds like it," Carina says.

"Now, see—I thought you didn't like kids," Dove says, pointing her fork at her.

"I didn't say I like them, I said this one little girl sounds cute."

"Okay, but doesn't that mean you like them?"

"Having the capacity to appreciate a cute kid does not equate to liking kids."

"I am *not* unemployed, Wesley!" Eddie chimes in, completely unrelated.

The conversation devolves into multiple simultaneous arguments. Wesley stands so quickly his knee bumps the table and he quickly heads out of the restaurant. Quinn tosses their cloth napkin onto the table and goes after him.

Quinn finds Wesley sitting on a bench just outside the entrance. "You okay?"

Wesley glances over and smiles. "Fine. Just got to be a little much in there."

Quinn stands awkwardly for a moment before sitting down beside him on the bench. They don't speak, just watching families as they walk into the restaurant. It stays like this for a few minutes, the two of them simply existing. It could almost feel like it used to—their comfortable silences. But this silence isn't quite as comfortable, quite as relaxing. It doesn't feel like home anymore.

Quinn realizes why they're so conflicted. It's like returning to burning rubble of a place you used to know. Wesley used to feel like home. Now all the stones are scorched and smoking.

After a while, Wesley pats his thighs and says, "We should go back in."

Quinn looks over at him. "Okay." Wesley's eyes look drained.

They stand and walk back into the restaurant and find their table again.

"Hey, you two!" Dove says, a look in her eyes that tells Quinn she thinks she won. She thinks they made up.

Did they?

Quinn thinks about the nice moments on the kayak, and about the lack of animosity just now. Maybe they did make up...

No. It's like Carina and kids: a lack of hatred doesn't equal love.

♪♪♪

Back at the house, Quinn realizes just how exhausted they are. The Florida sun seems to sap the life force from anyone who dares go outside for more than ten minutes at a time. They lay down on the couch and kick their feet up onto the arm, their head cushioned by about a hundred novelty throw pillows.

Quinn doesn't realize they've fallen asleep until they wake up to the sound of the front door closing. They look around sleepily, then notice Eddie standing in the dimly-lit kitchen. They can just see him through the peek-through.

"Hey, who just left?" Quinn asks, stretching.

"Mm," Eddie hums around a mouthful of something. Cereal, Quinn notes. "Wes. Said he'd be right back."

Quinn sits up and rubs their eyes. It's dark out now, and Quinn can hardly see anything out of the sliding glass door. The ocean is pitch black.

They say good night to Eddie, who is pouring himself another bowl of cereal. Quinn heads into their empty room and falls back asleep.

Quinn wakes up two more times—once when Eddie comes to bed groaning about being too full, and once when Wesley returns. Quinn is just awake enough to sense Wesley hovering over their bedside table. Then Wesley climbs into his own bed and Quinn doesn't remember anything after that.

They dream about kayaks, sharks, and pitch-black oceans.

♪♪♪

When they wake up in the morning, they remember it's the day of the Jamboree. They clear their throat and frown at how dry it is. They thought Florida was supposed to be super humid, perpetually damp.

Quinn reaches over for their water bottle and sees a paper bag on their bedside table. They pick up the bag and it's heavier than they thought. They notice it's stamped with the logo of the antique shop.

Inside is a note: *it can't replace the old pictures, but at least now you can take new ones.*

No way. Quinn takes out the newspaper-wrapped object and pulls aside the wrapping. It's the Canon AE-1 they saw at the shop. They turn it over in their hands, admiring the vintage strap attached to it, then test the battery and see there's a brand new one in it.

Quinn reaches back into the bag and pulls out a small yellow box—a new film canister. They open the packaging and take out the film, then flip open the back door of the camera and put it in. The door clicks shut and Quinn winds the film until it's ready to shoot.

They peer through the viewfinder and aim the camera at the window to their right, pressing the shutter button halfway to check the settings, then pressing it all the way to snap a picture. When Quinn pulls their eye away from the camera, they notice Wesley's empty bed.

He went out last night to get them an apology gift. Was the antique store even open that late?

Why would he go to all this trouble just to say sorry? Quinn thinks about Wesley's apology and Quinn's subsequent rejection and realizes that in their quest to avoid any conflict and confrontation, they've been thwarting Wesley's attempts at putting their animosity to rest for good. They both want the same thing.

Quinn sets the camera aside.

They get up and see that everyone but Dove is sitting in the living room or standing in the kitchen.

"Morning," Carina says.

Quinn smiles at her. They look at Wesley who's sitting on the couch, and they smile at him too.

Wesley's eyebrows shoot up and an honest grin spreads across his face. He shrinks it into a small smile, but his eyes retain their gleam.

"Ladies and gentlemen," a voice says from behind them—Dove. "It's the day of the 6th Annual Conch Republic Music Jamboree. Are you ready to make some music?" She's wearing a flowy wrap skirt with a lacy white bralette under a Hawaiian shirt. Her curls are pulled back into two poofs. She has big sunglasses that Quinn recognizes as Carina's.

Then Quinn realizes everyone has on a nice, beachy outfit. Carina is wearing an oversized black button-up tucked into the front of her shorts. She has stolen Basil's floppy sun hat again because apparently all Quinn's friends are thieves.

Quinn looks down at their pajamas. Time to change.

They head back into their room and dig through their suitcase. Their clothes are mostly black graphic tees that decidedly do not match the beachy aesthetic the group is going for. Quinn decides on their only light-colored shirt, an old, faded A Cademia tee from sectionals. The print is cracking and flaking from too many washes, and part of the lower hem is coming undone from picking at it, but they figure it works fine. Quinn crosses to the other room, roots around in Dove's suitcase, and finds a pair of white flowy shorts. Good enough.

When they walk back out, Dove says, "Hey, those are mine!" but she sounds more proud than angry.

"Wanna practice?" Wesley asks, and the group circles up. He plays their notes on his piano app and they sing through the song once, then twice, then three times. They keep running it until the harmony is exactly right. Quinn keeps accidentally making eye contact with Wesley from across the circle and they can feel themself blush each time.

"Alright, I think that's good," Wesley announces. *Finally.* It's only been a whole hour. "Ready?"

Quinn puts their hand out, and the rest follow suit, ready for the club cheer. "One... two... three!"

They each hit their note, and it sounds angelic.

"Let's go win this thing!" Basil yells, then lets out a deep, primal scream.

The rest of the group looks at each other in shock, then all at once, they each scream too.

Apparently, Key West turns out some pretty good musicians, because the performers that go before them are unfortunately really good.

After arriving and adding their group to the sign-up sheet, they stand in the crowd and watch the first performances.

A girl with a guitar sings an old Taylor Swift song that makes Dove cry. Three boys with a banjo, a fiddle, and a mandolin sing some country song, their voices blending into beautiful harmonies. An old man stands alone on the stage, leaning down to a too-short microphone stand, as a speaker plays the instrumental to a Jimmy Buffet song. His voice cracks in the most delightful, moody way.

Finally, they're up. They climb up the steps of the large gazebo and form a semicircle around the mic.

There aren't many people in the audience, and most of them have instruments of their own and are waiting for their own chance to perform. No one's rooting for them.

Quinn and Wesley are standing in the middle of the group, and Quinn lets their pinky brush Wesley's. He reaches his own out toward Quinn's hand, and they slowly tangle together. He almost feels like home again, but Quinn knows better.

CHAPTER 14
PAST

"We're here!" Dove sings as the minivan pulls to a stop in front of an auditorium. A large red banner hangs across the front that says '*Welcome singers!*' Large oak trees loom, scattered around by the entrance and in the medians between rows of parking spaces, and Dove parks the van in the shade of one of the larger ones.

They walk inside together and check in at the front desk. The woman confirms their time slot, then directs them to sit in a waiting room where a TV displays a live feed of the stage.

The group does vocal warm-ups quietly, unsure how much can be heard on the other side of the wall. Dove hops on one foot, alternating between her left and right while shaking out her arms and doing lip trill scales. Wesley is saying tongue twisters while Eddie and Basil practice a tricky harmony in one of their songs. Carina stands motionless.

Quinn watches her and notices her lips moving almost imperceptibly.

"What's she doing?" they ask Wesley quietly.

He leans down to whisper back, "She's running all the rhythms in her head at double the speed. In a minute, she'll run them backwards."

Quinn looks at her with a perfect mix of wonder and terror.

After they've all sufficiently warmed up, they sit in the black chairs along the wall and watch another university sing their hearts out. The soloist goes for the high note and her voice cracks.

"One down," Eddie says, high-fiving Dove.

"Hey," Wesley says in a warning voice. "Don't root for people to fail."

"But it gives us a better chance at winning."

"We don't want to win because other people are worse. We want to win because we're better."

As Quinn nods at the profound statement, Eddie whispers to Dove, "Isn't that the same thing?"

Not long after, it's their turn, and Quinn realizes they're nervous. They thought people only get nervous about things they care about. They frown as they think back through the last couple months. They've been working harder at getting this song right than they have at... anything so far.

They walk out of the small room and the woman directs them down a side hallway that connects to backstage. They stand at the edge of the side curtains. Quinn peers out at the audience and that was definitely a mistake because they're immediately filled with adrenaline and dread. They half want to back out of this whole thing and go home.

But they don't. When the judges finish writing and the announcer says their school name, they walk out and form a semicircle in the center of the stage. Quinn focuses on anything but the crowd.

Small mics are suspended from the ceiling. Quinn eyes the one closest to them and has the odd urge to yank it down. They pinch the bottom hem of their A Cademia tee instead.

Wesley takes out a little white rectangle that he's referred to as a chromatic pitch pipe and blows in one of the holes. From that, Quinn thinks their way up to their starting note, and on Wesley's count, the song begins.

As soon as their handmade music fills the room, Quinn's nerves spill out in the form of song, and when their voice melds perfectly with the others, any insecurity melts away, replaced by confidence only a singer can feel.

They finish their first song and kick into the second, which flies by. Finally, they sing their original arrangement of 'Persephone's Downfall'. Some of Quinn's nerves return. The judges have never heard this song sung by an a cappella group. They've probably never heard it at all. Quinn suggested this, and if the judges hate it and give them a terrible score because of it, it'll be Quinn's fault.

Carina begins her percussion and Basil, Dove, and Eddie form the perfect backdrop for Wesley and Quinn's melodies. Their notes bend and twist around each other, breaking at the peaks and drifting out into the audience. Any question now is gone. They're going to win.

Then Quinn's voice cracks.

The three colleges stand beside each other on the stage as the announcer finally gets to the results.

"Finishing in third place is..." He reads the card in his hand and says, "Copper Cove University."

The audience applauds lightly while Quinn's heart stops.

They look at Wesley's face—fallen, confused. Betrayed.

The six of them trudge off the stage as the announcer reveals the winner. Quinn watches as that group is handed a tall, silver trophy, all of them celebrating and hugging.

That would have been A Cademia if Quinn hadn't ruined this.

CHAPTER 15
PRESENT

Their voices ring out in the Key West plaza as they sing their heavy metal doo-wop. The arrangement has a forward rhythm that sounds the way skipping feels, and Eddie, Dove, and Basil's background harmonies flow like the river they spent yesterday afternoon exploring.

Quinn and Wesley sing perfectly together, their notes twisting around each other just like they did four months ago. They sing lyrics about murdering Hades, then wondering if she made the right decision as she eats another messy pomegranate.

Somehow, it works. It really works.

♩♩♩

As the host announces the winners, Quinn flashes back to that stage last semester. They close their eyes tight and pick at the hem of their shirt.

Wesley won't forgive them twice… if he even forgave them once.

They hear their group name called, and Quinn is sure they've just been told they lost, but when their friends squeal and celebrate, they realize—*they won*. They climb the steps of the gazebo, and the announcer hands them an envelope containing information about the condo prize, but all Quinn sees is a tall, silver trophy instead.

Quinn glances at Wesley and smiles.

They arrive at the condo and Dove ceremoniously unlocks the door. "Enter, my children!"

The group rushes in and Quinn's friends call dibs on bedrooms. There are four this time instead of two.

Quinn lugs their suitcase across the threshold of the front door and leaves it in the living room before exploring the condo. Straight ahead is a couch and TV, and beyond it, a sliding glass door that leads onto a balcony overlooking the beach. To their right is a bathroom with bedrooms on either side of it. There are two twin beds in the furthest-back bedroom. To Quinn's left is the kitchen, and back towards the front door are two more bedrooms.

"Hey, Dove, didn't they say this place sleeps six?"

Dove walks closer to them from one of the rooms. "Yeah. One, two, three, four, five…" she counts as she points to the beds. She thinks for a moment. "Oh, six. Sleeper sofa."

Quinn rushes to call dibs on a room before they're left sleeping on the pull-out bed. They end up in the back bedroom with the two twin beds. They leave their luggage there, then notice the room has its own balcony entrance. They open the sliding glass door and step out.

They watch as kids play, some running around at the shoreline, some digging a hole in the wet sand. A very red man sleeps face down on his beach towel. A woman sits under an umbrella and reads.

The ocean is a deep teal blue today, and a few clouds cast shadows on the water. The waves build, crest, and crash long before they reach the shore. By that time, they're slowly carrying foam to the sand, tickling at beachgoers' feet.

The sliding glass door opens behind them, and Wesley joins them in leaning on the railing. He must have chosen the other bed in this room. He's silent for a while, watching the people down below too. Then he says, "You should be proud.

That's the best you've ever sung. Your voice didn't crack this time. Nice work."

Everything Quinn's been trying to forget comes flooding back.

CHAPTER 16
PAST

They walk out into the parking lot, energy much different from when they arrived. Even Dove walks slowly, like she's in a fog.

Eddie tries to crack a joke, but no one has the energy to laugh.

The ride to their university is short, thankfully, but it feels impossibly long.

Dove parks at her dorm hall, so Quinn says goodbye and sets off toward their own. Wesley is walking up ahead of them, and Quinn catches up. They reach out for his hand, but he moves it away.

"Wes?"

"Don't call me that."

Quinn gapes at him. "Wesley—"

"I was so stupid. So stupid."

"What? No, it's *my* voice that cracked. It's my—"

"I should have known when you got a C on that easy-as-hell paper. This is why I hate tutoring."

"What does that have to do with anything? Wesley—"

Wesley stops walking and finally faces them, but Quinn wishes he didn't. His eyes are cold and stormy, and the line between his eyebrows is deep. His voice, however, is soft. "It's my fault, Quinn. I should have known you weren't cut out for this. You didn't even warm up with everyone else."

"I warmed up before we got there."

"Your voice cracked."

"I was nervous. It was my first performance."

Wesley turns away and keeps walking.

Anger fills Quinn's gut, replacing the shock and sting of Wesley's words. Quinn rushes to catch up and grabs Wesley's elbow. "If I failed the club, it's only because you didn't lead well enough."

"You were supposed to apply yourself."

"It wouldn't matter if I did or not. Same with that C I got. You were supposed to help me. So—so it's your fault."

"Help yourself. Walk away."

"But—my dorm's that way."

"Walk away, Quinn. Before I say something I'll regret."

Quinn stops walking. "Like what?"

Wesley stops, turns, shakes his head. Twists the knife. "You're a failure. You failed the group, you nearly failed your stupid paper—and you definitely would have without me." Wesley scoffs.

"That's not true. You're the one who failed. You were supposed to help me. You were supposed to—You said you could love me."

"Love you?" Wesley smirks, and it's an awful, ugly, lopsided thing. "Look at these pictures."

Then he snatches Quinn's camera and for one horrible moment, they think he's about to break it. Then he does something worse.

He opens the back door and light floods in, ruining the film. "They're just—"

"No!" Quinn cries.

Wesley's entire demeanor changes and he slams the back shut again. "What?" he says, panic creeping into his voice.

"You ruined it! You ruined the film! They can't touch light till they're developed." Quinn snatches the camera back, and tears sting at their eyes. "Why would you do that?"

"I didn't mean—I was just trying to look at them."

"You can't see them when they're not developed yet, dipshit!"

"I didn't know. You didn't tell me that."

"I didn't think I'd have to."

"Quinn—"

"*You* walk away," Quinn says dangerously.

Wesley does, and gradually he's reduced to the sound of receding footsteps.

Quinn stares down at the camera in their hands, the back still hanging half open. There's no saving these photos.

There's no saving any of this.

CHAPTER 17
PRESENT

"Why would you say that?"

Wesley looks stunned. "Say what?"

"That my voice didn't crack. Why would you bring that up?"

"I didn't mean anything by it. I just—"

"You just what? Thought bringing up that day would be fine?"

"That day? What—" Then he gets it. Wesley's eyes go wide with what almost looks like fear. "Quinn, I didn't mean to—"

Wesley was about to say what might have been a very nice apology, but Quinn interrupts. It's their turn to hurt him.

"You don't even understand what you did, do you? You're so smart, such a scholar, a tutor, but you can't even see the damage you did. You took something I loved, and you destroyed it."

"The film?"

"No, dipshit. Us."

Wesley looks away.

"You—you broke us up over, what? My voice cracking? Fuck you."

"Quinn, that's not—"

"Not what? Fair? I could say a lot more and a lot worse, and it'd still be fair."

"No—Would you just listen to me? For one second?" Wesley exclaims, hands on his head.

Quinn is silent, but only out of shock, not obedience.

"I put everything I had, everything I *was,* into that group. I brought you into it. Do you understand that? I saw something in you that made me add you to the only thing that ever brought me any fucking joy. You. Something about *you.*"

Quinn twists the hem of their shirt.

"And I watched you mangle it. You skipped practices, you lip-synced, you goofed off, and you messed it all up. You fucked everything up!"

"My voice cracked!" Quinn shouts back.

"I knew your voice would crack. I'm the one that gave you that note!" Then Wesley says again, softer, "I'm the one that gave you that note."

Quinn watches as Wesley falls apart.

He leans on the railing of the balcony, silent, still, except for the quick rise and fall of his shoulders.

Finally, he looks at Quinn again. "I did this."

"Yeah, you did," Quinn agrees bitterly.

"No, I—I *did* this. I knew what would happen, and—I always do this. When things are good, I get in my own way. With tutoring, with the club, with—" Wesley's eyes go soft. "With you." He steps closer, and his hand covers Quinn's own on the railing. "I'm so sorry, Quinn. For everything. For what happened, for this trip, for—for all of it."

Quinn turns back toward the ocean, toward the people laying out on the sand, unaware of Wesley rending Quinn's heart from their body once again. They take a breath, turn back to Wesley, and mutter, "Save it."

Quinn pushes off the railing and walks back inside, closing the sliding glass door behind them. They pull the curtains shut, not wanting to see Wesley for a single second longer than they have to.

Quinn turns to walk into the rest of the villa and nearly yelps when they see Carina standing in the doorway.

She uncrosses her arms and steps forward. Quinn can't hold it together any longer, and they fall into her.

"It's okay, Canon," she says quietly, petting their hair. "It's all okay."

"Quinn, come have leftover cake with us!" Basil calls from the kitchen.

"Come on, bud," Carina says. She takes their hand and leads them out of the room.

A few minutes into staining their mouth with blue frosting, the sliding glass door opens, and Quinn hears Wesley fumble with the curtains.

"You okay?" Eddie asks quietly from the barstool next to Quinn's.

"Fine," they reply.

Why would Wesley bring all this up, then expect forgiveness? The best Quinn could give him on this trip was cordiality. How can he expect anything more than that?

"Quinn," Dove says, and they look up. "C'mere." She nods her head toward the front bedroom and Quinn follows.

They sit together on the side of the bed, and she places a hand on their knee. "What went on in there?"

Quinn falls backward onto the bed, arms flung out. After a long, drawn-out groan, they say, "He brought up all that shit from last semester, then turned it around so he's the fucking victim, and then had the nerve to say sorry as if that fixes anything."

Dove's brows knit together. "He said he's the victim? What do you mean?"

Quinn leans up on their elbows. "He didn't say that exactly. He had this revelation or whatever. Says he sabotages himself and that my voice cracking was his fault, not mine."

"Okay…"

"Well—then he got all sad about it like I was supposed to comfort *him*." Quinn looks at Dove as if to say, 'isn't that crazy?' but she just keeps looking at them like they're a puzzle she's trying to solve.

"Quinn," she starts, and they don't like where this is going. "I love you. You know I love you." *Oh, god.* Nothing good ever starts this way. "But you're kind of being an idiot."

Quinn's jaw drops with incredulity.

"Listen—That guy in there messed up. Bad. He hurt you, and of course that's not okay. But is he really playing the victim? Or did he realize something devastating about himself, see what he did wrong, and try to make it right?"

Quinn frowns and mutters, "The second one."

"I'm not to say you owe him forgiveness. You can stay mad forever if you want. That's totally up to you. I'm just saying... don't write him off just for that. I don't think he's trying to play the victim. I think he's just saying he cares." Dove slings her arms around them and hugs them tightly before standing to leave. As she reaches the doorway, she adds, "You should have seen how he's been looking at you this week."

"Like he hates me?" Quinn bites.

"No. Quite the opposite." Dove winks and walks out, leaving Quinn to slump back down and watch the ceiling fan twirl.

They let out another groan. What does that even mean? The opposite of hate. That guy in there doesn't love him.

Did he ever?

♪♪♪

Quinn jolts awake to Eddie smacking them on the stomach over and over.

"Up and at 'em!" Eddie shouts.

"Is it morning?" Quinn asks blearily.

"No, it's, like, 4 AM."

"Why'd you wake me up?"

"This is my room," Eddie answers.

"Then why are you just now coming to bed?"

"I was busy."

"Doing what?" Quinn sits up and stretches as Eddie slides under the covers.

"Pondering. A boy's gotta ruminate sometimes, you know?"

"Oh, of course." Quinn has always enjoyed Eddie's zaniness. There's always a seed of wisdom in every odd statement. "Hey, Eddie," Quinn starts.

"At your service."

"Are you quick to forgive?"

Eddie thinks about this for a moment, then says, "You know, I've never forgiven anyone before."

"Really? You don't seem the type to hold grudges."

"No, no—I definitely don't hold grudges. What I mean is... I've never felt like anyone really needed to apologize for anything. People do what they do. What's meant to happen will happen. If someone does something wrong, it's just there to help me on my way, you know? So they're just playing their part. No harm in that."

Quinn nods. "You've really never been mad at anyone?"

Eddie laughs from deep in his chest. "Ooh yes, I have. Listen—Have I told you this? Eh, I'm gonna tell you again. So there was this guy, Thad. Whose name is Thad, anyway? Okay, so..."

Eddie goes on to tell a story about a guy in his first semester of college who cheated off Eddie's paper and caused them both to fail. That was Eddie's last chance to pull up his grade, so he ended up having to retake the class. He was furious and for good reason. But during his retake, he met Basil, who introduced him to the a cappella club, which caused him to change his major to music.

"If I hadn't failed that class, my whole life would have been on a different trajectory. I could have been hit by a bus by now or maybe even joined a cult. I don't know. Who knows what Thad could have saved me from?"

"So you're saying Wesley breaking my heart happened for a reason?"

"Ooh, this is about Wes?"

Quinn nods.

"You should do what you feel is right. If you want to forgive him, do it. If you don't want to, don't. If you want to live free like me and accept whatever path you're on, totally do that. It's all up to you." Eddie grasps Quinn's shoulder and looks into their eyes intensely. "Only you... can choose what you do. Got it?"

Quinn grimaces. "Since when do you write inspirational posters?"

Eddie laughs, laying back down. "Maybe I should get into that. I think I'd be pretty good at it."

"I think you would, Ed." Quinn flicks Eddie's toe through the blanket. "Thanks."

"Any time, young one."

Quinn walks out of the room and flicks the light off. Immediately, they hear snoring.

Eddie's an odd bird, but he's a lovely one.

Quinn walks back into the main area of the villa and sees the dark ocean through the sliding glass door. They walk over to it and are about to step out onto the balcony when they hear a small voice say, "Quinn?"

They turn and see Basil sitting up on the pull-out bed.

"Are you okay?" she asks, blinking and rubbing her eyes.

"Fine, Bas. Go back to sleep."

"It's okay if you're not," Basil says. She shifts to the right and pats the empty spot next to her on the bed.

Quinn lays down and rests their head on her pillow. Basil settles in with her cheek on their shoulder.

"I love you," she says quietly.

Quinn quirks an eyebrow. "I love you too, bud."

"It's been really nice having all of us back together again, hasn't it?"

"For sure," Quinn says with a smile.

"Sorry if Wesley being here kind of made it more tense for you."

"Not at all. This week's about you, anyway. Doesn't matter that he's here. No tension at all."

"Well, I've been watching you two all week. I'm pretty sure there's tension." She lifts her head to look at them. Quinn expects her to comment on the unpleasant bitterness, but she means a different kind of tension. "The way you two look at each other... Wow."

"I don't *look* at him," Quinn scoffs.

"When you aren't glaring, you do. Your eyes go all soft like they used to. Gooey," Basil teases.

"You need to get your eyes checked."

"Okay," she says, resting her head again. "I could be wrong." Basil's quiet for a while, letting Quinn consider her observation. Then she says, "This has been such a good trip. Thanks for coming."

"Wouldn't miss it."

A few moments later, she's softly snoring, and Quinn gently scooches out from under her cheek.

They stand up and cross to the sliding glass door, stepping out into the warm air.

Quinn thought it would be quieter out here, but at night, the ocean waves roar.

They take a deep breath of salty sea air, then let it out slowly. They *so* don't look at him.

Time for a mental list.

Reasons Not to Forgive Wesley:
1. He's a dipshit.
2. He broke Quinn's heart.
3. He made his apology all about himself.
4. He's a dipshit.

Quinn moves to the other side of the balcony and peers through the sliding glass door into their and Wesley's room.

Through a gap in the curtains, Quinn can see him. He's on his side facing the far wall. Quinn is about to look away, realizing how creepy this is, when Wesley turns over and Quinn sees he's wide awake.

His face is tense, eyebrows drawn and lips twisting in a deep frown. He scrubs his hands over his cheeks and sits up, throwing his legs over the opposite side of the bed and hunching forward on his elbows.

Wesley's shoulders start to shake.

Quinn turns away.

Wesley changed Quinn's life. He introduced them to their friends, showed them how to engage with music in a brand-new way, and it has enriched them every single day.

Wesley put them on this path. Quinn wouldn't have found it on their own.

And he tried to take accountability for the fight, but Quinn just didn't let him.

Wesley destroyed Quinn's heart. He ripped it open and ruined its film. But maybe it's not all ruined.

Quinn walks back to the other sliding glass door and steps quietly into the living room. They tap lightly on the door to their bedroom before pushing it open and stepping in.

"Quinn," Wesley says, sitting straight up and wiping roughly at his eyes.

"I could forgive you," Quinn says plainly.

"What?"

"I said I could forgive you."

"Why?"

Quinn hadn't been expecting that question. "Because you said sorry."

"You don't have to forgive me if I don't deserve it."

Quinn looks at Wesley, sees his tired, reddened eyes, the heavy slope of his shoulders, his fingers hanging limply across his knees, nails bitten to the bed.

"Well, are you sorry?"

"Of course. Quinn, I am so goddamn sorry. I never should have said any of that to you before, never should have brought it up this time. Even that camera I got you, that was too far, I—"

Quinn steps closer and says, "I could forgive you, Wes. Really." They close the gap between them and stand between Wesley's knees.

Wesley raises his hands but doesn't touch Quinn until Quinn leans down and hugs him first.

Wesley sucks in a breath. "I'll be better. I promise. I'll be the best friend you can imagine."

Quinn pulls back and smiles at him. "You'd better be."

The sun streams in and finds the pair still awake, laying side by side, conversation flowing like the ocean outside.

Quinn has one leg draped over Wesley's as they tell the story of the worst professor they ever had.

"And I finally got my grade up to an 89.9%, and the man wouldn't round it up to an A."

"No," Wesley says, invested.

"I know right? And—" Quinn glances over at Wesley and sees his expression a split second before Wesley glances away. "What?"

"What-what?" Wesley asks.

"What's with the face?"

"The face?"

"Yeah. The ooey gooey face you were making at me."

"Just smiling."

"Uh-huh." Quinn narrows their eyes. "So *that's* the look."

"The look?"

"Mm-hm. Carina told me you've been *looking* at me. With the 'opposite of hate', she said."

Wesley laughs. "Love?"

"You tell me."

He looks at them with that expression again, smiling gently and easily, eyes half-lidded and glowing. "Maybe."

Quinn's breath catches in their throat.

Wesley reaches out and touches Quinn's arm, fingertips brushing over their skin as softly as humanly possible. "Is that okay?"

Quinn can only nod.

Wesley sits up. Quinn does too.

He leans on one arm, raises the other to touch the side of Quinn's jaw, leans in, and forgiveness goes out the window.

Quinn doesn't forgive him. Wesley doesn't need to be forgiven.

He put them on this path. The one that leads to kissing a hot man that loves them while listening to the ocean in the Florida Keys.

"Is this okay?" Wesley breathes.

Quinn nods and surges forward again.

Eventually, they break apart, and Quinn speaks so quietly they're not sure if Wesley can hear them, saying, "I could love you. I think."

"You could?" Wesley says, a smile boosting his cheeks up to his eyes.

"Yeah. I could." Quinn smiles softly up at him.

Wesley presses their foreheads together. "I could love you, too."

The end of Basil's birthday trip came quicker than anticipated, and before they knew it, the group was headed their separate ways. They all still live within a couple of hours of the university, but only Basil, Dove, and Quinn would return for classes at the start of the semester.

Wesley's graduated status doesn't keep him from visiting, though. He's in Quinn's dorm, lying flat on his back in Quinn's twin bed while they sit at their desk filling out a worksheet for Psych 2. They don't even consult the textbook. Something about this subject just clicks.

They finish the last question, then look over at Wesley who's rereading *Lord of the Flies*.

"Do you ever miss college?" Quinn asks.

Wesley looks over, then closes the book and sits up. Quinn sits down next to him.

"Only sometimes," Wesley says. "I miss you,"—he gives them a kiss on the nose—"I miss essays."

"What?" Quinn exclaims with a laugh.

"And I miss the club," Wesley admits.

"I'm sorry I messed up your last performance," Quinn says. They aren't sure if that emotional bruise will ever heal.

Wesley shushes them. "Sectionals wasn't my last performance. And you have nothing to be sorry for." Wesley sighs. "I don't know. I just miss the team, I guess. No a cappella group will ever be the same as when it was the six of us."

Quinn supposes he's right. It was nice to have a built-in friend group working towards a common goal and creating music together. *What if...* Quinn looks at him and smiles.

♪♪♪

"Guys, we have a special guest today. He's gonna help us work on our breath support since that judge told us our 'tone lacks intensity,'" Quinn says to the group of freshmen and sophomores, and they laugh at the memory of that stuck-up judge.

The special guest pecks Quinn on the cheek before walking up to the front of the black box theater.

"Wesley's not a special guest anymore," one student says.

"He's here so often, he might as well be part of the club again!" another student jokes.

Quinn smiles and joins Basil and Dove standing at the side of the room.

This is the biggest the a cappella club has ever been since it began six or seven years ago, and all it took was offering to tutor a bunch of freshmen in psychology in exchange for their singing voices.

Quinn smiles as they watch Wesley teach the club about proper breathing techniques.

They're glad their poor essay skills led them here, to Wesley.

Quinn could love him.

No. They already do.

ABOUT the AUTHOR

Connor Bryan began writing stories in 2nd grade with a crayon-illustrated series entitled *Cat and Mouse*. Her passion for writing never left her and developed into a love of poetry and fiction. She writes and lives in central Florida. To learn more about Connor and her writing, please visit connorbryanwrites.com or follow @conbryanwrites on Instagram, Twitter, and TikTok.

Also by Connor Bryan:

JACK FINCH BELIEVES IN GHOSTS